## MISTS OF MENACE—

In alternating steam heat and mountain chill, we made our way to the edge of the clearing and the belching white-shading-to-pink cone. As we got closer, I saw the small volcano was perhaps fifteen feet high with an irregular crater from which the vapor blew before twining mistily away.

I stared at it with a mixture of fear and marvel, and wondered fearfully if the girl beside me now had led my sister here to a fateful rendezvous.

Suddenly I felt my companion's presence vanish. She was gone! Vanished like the vapors that came and went in this weird, secluded valley. Had she left me to find my way or wander forever, lost in the ever-present fog until I should stumble to some scalding doom? Or was this evil demon-child even now creeping up behind me through the mists, arms outstretched for a final, deadly push . . . ?

# THE
# WINTER
# KEEPER

*Jeanne Williams*
*writing as Jeanne Crecy*

AN AUTHORS GUILD BACKINPRINT.COM EDITION

**FOR PAULINE**
Wise and good, my friend

# 1

Mother naturally believed the telegram Anne sent from Montana saying that she had won Smoke Valley Lodge's annual prize for best helper of the season, a holiday at Long Beach. Mother also believed the telegram arriving a week later, which said that Anne had been surfing, slipped, and had drowned. That message was signed by a Lars Nordstrom, who identified himself as a friend.

When we tried to find out more, the Long Beach police could not locate such a man, nor could they find any registration for Anne at any of the hotels or resorts, though they did find one for Mr. and Mrs. Lars Nordstrom, who had taken a luxury suite near the beach for a week. And they did report an unidentified body washed up on the beach, which answered Anne's description. I flew out to identify her, hoping till that last second that the drowned girl would be someone else. But she was Anne, terribly gashed and broken, and her body came home for burial on the same plane I flew. The police sent out a pick-up call for Nordstrom, but it brought no results, and I had the feeling they were too busy to pursue the riddle beyond routine measures.

After the funeral Mother wrote Nordstrom's alleged home address in Minnesota. The letter was returned with "no such town" written on it, and person-to-person phone calls to both Smoke Valley Lodge, Montana, and Minnesota brought no results. The owner of Smoke Valley Lodge, however, did talk to Mother, and delivered a blow that left Mother shattered. She stared at me unseeingly as she put down the phone.

"Mrs. Lindsay says that—that Anne was fired for—for misbehaving with this Nordstrom," Mother said, after I brought her a glass of water and she could speak. "She says they left the lodge together and she can only suppose that Anne didn't want us to know what she was doing. Mrs. Lindsay hated to tell me—she did it as gently as she could. She liked Anne and was terribly upset when she started neglecting her job to be with Nordstrom. Mrs. Lindsay says she talked frankly with Anne several times; she had hoped Anne would stay through the winter when they need only one woman at the lodge to keep things going."

"That kind of thing just doesn't sound like Anne," I managed, when I could say anything.

Mother fiddled with her wedding ring, the one she'd had from Anne's father, Jack Dupree, a charming lazy rascal she'd married after my father died. I could barely remember Dupree. He had deserted our family when Anne was two and I was four. Since then, mother had supported us by selling real estate in our home town of St. Louis, Missouri. She was better off now than when she was with Dupree, because then she'd had to subsidize him also. She still looked amazingly young at forty-five, with ash-blonde hair piled into a French knot, and only tiny wrinkles about the eyes to betray any sign of aging in her smooth, fair skin.

Anne resembled her, while I, from pictures, obviously inherited my father's rather long face, straight dark eyebrows, and thick black hair. I had taken after him in figure, too, dismayingly, and even though no one took me for a boy anymore as they had during my early teens, I had grown up envying Anne's sweet curves, her delectable femininity.

"No," said Mother, slowly calming dow. "It doesn't sound like Anne. But after all, she's scarcely twenty." Mother spoke as if Anne were alive, but I didn't correct her. I, too, couldn't accept that bubbling, gay, affectionate Anne could be dead.

"Anne had boys hanging around her in swarms, Mother! And at school—" Anne and I had both gone to the state university—"well, you should have seen it. Knee-deep in both football players and Phi Beta Kappa types!"

"Still, they were all *boys*," Mother said impatiently. "Nordstrom, according to Mrs. Lindsay, is a wealthy sportsman in his thirties. It's possible he turned Anne's head ..."

Mother twisted her ring again, remembering, I didn't doubt, how Anne's father had turned *her* head, and perhaps fearing, wondering if Jack Dupree had bequeathed to Anne a streak of latent folly and recklessness.

My memories of Anne, laced though they were with painful comparisons between the two of us, didn't hold anything that made me think Anne would neglect her job, or go off with a playboy lover. Even assuming that she might have done so, the first telegram's lie seemed unlike Anne and totally superfluous.

"If Anne did go to Long Beach with Nordstrom," I said, thinking aloud, "I don't think she'd have sent that kind of explanation. She'd just have said she was with a friend, probably phoned or sent a card."

Or, if she were ashamed of what she was doing, or beglamored out of her senses, she might not have let us know anything.

"I don't know what to do," Mother said, watching me with enormous blue eyes so like Anne's that pain squeezed my heart tight. "The Long Beach police say they'll watch for Nordstrom and any other clues, but there are a good many drownings, some never reported."

"Nordstrom owes us more than a telegram," I said. "He's the witness. Why didn't he call the police? What if he's lying? For that matter, does he even exist?"

"He was registered at the hotel," Mother said. "And Mrs. Lindsay says he's been vacationing at Smoke Valley for five or six years."

"But his Minnesota address isn't right." Mother and I looked at each other. Then we got out an atlas and hunted through Minnesota town names. We found nothing even close to the alleged place Nordstrom had given as his home.

"Maybe," ventured Mother, "we ought to put a detective after this man. For Anne to drown like that according to someone who uses a false address—well, I'm not ready to leave it there!"

It made a ferocious dent in her savings, but Mother got a private investigation bureau after Lars Nordstrom. After a month, and trips to Long Beach, Smoke Valley Lodge and Minnesota, the investigator, a nice middle-aged widower named Michael McShane, had found nothing more than Mrs. Lindsay had already told us. Nordstrom, while at Smoke Valley Lodge, kept to himself. He drove a rental car. And the rental car company had the same fake address as we did.

The Long Beach police were still watching for fresh information, of course, but there was nothing new from them. Anne's body had been too ruined for them to tell if she had drowned, if there had been water in her lungs.

McShane looked really distressed and sympathetic when he told us the results of his search. And I thought the way he touched Mother's shoulder was more than a routine gesture of comfort, though I was too preoccupied with Anne to give it much thought.

An idea was forming in my mind—daring, frightening, but at least a possible way to find out if there was anything concealed about Anne's death.

My summer job with a Head Start program was over. I had been pondering whether to go back to school for my Master's in Education or get a job in St. Louis so I could stay with Mother during what was a heartbreaking time. But so long as we couldn't be sure we knew the whole truth about Anne's death, we couldn't mourn her and let her go. Instead, anxiety about something hidden plagued us both.

"Mother," I said abruptly, "didn't Mrs. Lindsay say they needed a girl at the lodge through the winter?"

"Why, yes. That's why she hated to see Anne go."

"I think maybe I'll be that girl!"

McShane looked startled. "Janet!" Mother said, using my whole name which meant she was upset, just as Anne's real name, Annette, was only used under stress. "You were planning on going back to school. Besides, after—after Anne, I'd be worried about you!"

"I'm about as much like Anne as a cactus is like a rose," I scoffed. "No mysterious lover's going to abscond with me! If we're to learn about Anne, it seems to be up to us. Nordstrom hasn't left any real tracks in either Minnesota or Long Beach, but he apparently is a steady guest at Smoke Valley. If I spent the winter there, I might find out a good deal."

"But—"

I put my arms around my mother, realizing how fragile she was physically, though she never acted tired. "Please, Mother, let me try! I—I really couldn't study, wondering if I couldn't have learned something. I do hate to leave you here, but I'd write often and phone sometimes—not collect, either!" I teased, trying to grin and cheer us both up.

Mother sighed, stroking my hair absent-mindedly. After a while, she said, "You *will* be careful, darling?"

"To the point of cowardice," I promised. "And I won't even have to lie about my name since Anne's and mine are different."

Mother's lips tucked down a bit wryly. "Always looking on the bright side! And our letters to Anne always went under my name. But how will you apply for the job without letting on that you're Anne's sister?"

"I'll just write and say a friend was entranced with Smoke Valley and I thought maybe they could use someone for the winter—if not, could I please have a job next summer? Sounds valid, doesn't it?"

"I suppose so." But Mother didn't look convinced. She turned involuntarily to Michael McShane. His shrewd dark eyes gave me a weighing look.

"You *might* learn something," he conceded. "But you'd have to be mighty cautious. And you must promise to let me know if you run into trouble."

"Thanks," I said. "You can bet I will."

Without being told, I was sure he'd be seeing Mother, and that was good.

I gave for my return address in my application that of a friend who lived in a small town outside St. Louis. Mrs. Lindsay responded by return mail. If I understood that the lodge was lonesome in the winter—in fact, I'd be there all by myself, for she and her husband lived in their own house a few miles from the lodge—then I was welcome to the job, and would have first choice of summer positions except for the cook's, who spent winters in Florida but migrated North for the season.

Mrs. Lindsay asked me to telephone her at once, if I wanted the work, and urged me to come as soon as possible, since snow fell early in the mountains and it would be best for me to be settled in comfortably before winter came.

Mid-September in St. Louis was still warm, but after phoning that I'd take the job, I packed my winter clothes and caught a plane to Billings, Montana, the nearest airport to Smoke Valley, which lay between Billings and Yellowstone National Park just over in Wyoming. Anne had gone to Yellowstone several times, but had written that she preferred to wander about Smoke Valley, thus named for its geysers, hot springs, and bubbling fumaroles, because there she could see the same kind of marvels that attracted hordes to Yellowstone—but without the hordes.

"I've got my own pet geyser," she had proudly informed us. "He's a whitish cone that rumbles and bubbles and erupts about every hour or so, sort of a little volcano that spews steam instead of lava. And not far from Suvi—that's short for Vesuvius!—are colored mud springs that bubble, bubble, toil and trouble! I hope I can stay here after the season; the Lindsays always have got one winter keeper, and it must be gorgeous when snow covers everything and people have to get about on snowmobiles. Mrs. Lindsay has one and has promised to teach me how to use it . . ."

The winter keeper.

I wondered, as the plane came jarring down on the runway, where this winter would be keeping my younger sister. Was her laughter, her bright, dancing personality really gone? It didn't seem possible. It seemed that so much energy had to exist still somewhere, even though her slender body was underground forever.

I braced against the jolting vibration of the plane's dash down the runway and tried to assure myself that I was doing the best thing in order to try to learn the truth about Anne. But that didn't quiet nervous spasms in my stomach as I deplaned, passed through the entrance doors, and looked about for Mrs. Lindsay.

What would she be like? *Very beautiful*, Anne had once noted. *Not happy, though.* Irritatingly, she had scratched out the rest of the paragraph. That was like Anne, who abhorred gossip, but it had frustrated both Mother and me.

Mrs. Lindsay and I had agreed that our key to recognition would be my red trenchcoat, a dashing belted affair with lots of gilt buttons and a shoulder cape. One good thing about being tall and skinny—my wrists had always seemed to be poking out under my sleeves as I grew up—was that I could wear bulky things without looking plump.

"You lucky beast!" Anne had once adjured when she reluctantly decided a plaid skirt made her hips seem too broad. "You can wear plaids and horizontal stripes and big splashy patterns. And even get away with a picture hat without looking like some stumpy little mushroom."

"Well, lollipop," I had replied wryly, "I don't *like* picture hats and splashy patterns. And I could wrap the tartans of every clan in Scotland around me, but I'll bet the most ardent Highlander would break his neck passing me up to get at you!"

"Not when your real man comes along," Anne said soberly. "And you really wouldn't want to waste time with a flock of others."

"Easy for you to say," I replied dourly. "Pushing one's way—just once—through a shoal of admirers would be a mind-enlarging experience, and I think every girl should have it."

"Mind-blowing," teased Anne. She eyed me thoughtfully. "There are thousands of girls who look like me—curvy, bloom of youth, and all that. At fifty we'll be pleasant buxom matrons fighting double chins and flab. But you, darn you, will still have that subtle, fascinating lean and hungry look. Sort of sculptured." Anne gave a decided shake of her head. "You may not get as many fellows as I do, sister sweet, but the ones you attract will be really mad about *you*, not just turned on by a sunny smile. By the way, it would help if you didn't *glower* at men when they make stupid remarks. They can't all be smart."

Just then her date drove up in his sleek new Stingray. She blew me a kiss and strolled down the walk arm in arm with a black-haired six-footer who had almost made the Olympic swim team and was doing all right in law school, too.

I went out for a scintillating evening at the library, but if anyone there was smitten with my subtle lean look, they managed to conceal it.

Dear, kind, blessed Anne! What had happened to her? Had she loved this Nordstrom?

I stood by the railing of the gate and looked around for a woman who might seem to be watching for someone. There were several such, but they ignored my red coat and happily greeted other passengers, bearing them off like trophies snatched from our gargantuan travel system.

Gradually, no one else was left. I stood there alone, worrying about my baggage and where, oh where, Mrs. Lindsay was.

Five minutes. Ten.

Smoke Valley was ninety miles away. There could have been all kinds of delays. I flagged a skycap and gave him my baggage stubs, explaining the problem. He promised to collect my baggage and stow it in a safe place till I came for it. One worry settled, but I was getting hungry.

Very hungry. I had managed to change planes in such a way that I hadn't been served a single meal all day, or even had time to grab a snack in some terminal. All I had consumed since breakfast was a glass of milk, two ginger ales, and a packet of salted nuts. It was now four-thirty. I had always possessed the appalling appetite common to many thin people, and now it was raging.

Perhaps there was a misunderstanding about arrival time. Or maybe Mrs. Lindsay had had a flat tire or an accident. I paced around the gate, looking at my watch every few minutes, and decided, when Mrs. Lindsay was a half-hour late, that I'd better phone the lodge.

There were phone booths at the end of the corridor, and I could watch the gate while I phoned. If a woman appeared, I would intercept her before she could leave.

Once in the phone booth, I got out the letter with the Smoke Valley phone number, dialed, inserted the requested coins, and, with a strange, sinking, deserted feeling, heard the phone ring and ring and ring.

I was just about to hang up when the receiver on the other end lifted and a child's voice, thin and unsexed, demanded, "What do you want?"

Startled, I caught my breath before I said, "Is Mrs. Lindsay there, please?"

"No, she's not," returned the voice unhelpfully.

"Well, maybe you could give somebody a message. Mrs. Lindsay was supposed to meet me at the airport. She's quite late."

"She always is," said the child. "And my father's gone, too, so you'll just have to wait, I suppose."

"But—"

There was a click. I sat staring at the buzzing receiver, fighting vexed tears. Rude little so-and-so! The Lindsay's child? If so, it was a good thing the lodge and residence were separate.

Should I call back? Insist on talking to some adult? Before I could decide, a form blocked the booth window. I glanced up to encounter the angry gray eyes of a tall man in a sheepskin coat and cream-colored Stetson.

He yanked the door of the booth open. I involuntarily flinched back, wondering if he were crazy, my mouth half-open to scream.

"There you are!" he said harshly. "Lucky that red coat showed through the glass." As I still stood there and gaped at him, he caught my arm. "Come along!" he ordered. "I've wasted enough time this afternoon."

## 2

I am usually a mild-mannered person, but being shouted at, seized, and dragged around was too much on top of ravening hunger, a long wait, and a nasty kid on the telephone. I caught the wall of the phone booth and dug in my heels. Literally.

"Just a minute!" I breathed. "Since you know about my coat, you must be from Smoke Valley, but exactly who are you? And what right have you to haul me out of a phone booth after I've been waiting for almost forty-five minutes? Wouldn't you have tried to find out what was wrong if you were in my shoes?"

He glanced from his big scuffed rawhide boots to my crinkle-patent copper-colored pumps. His long mouth slanted reluctantly. He really looked at me for the first time. I looked at him, too, and decided that he had a good, strong face except for when wrath turned it craggy. I was still very much on my dignity, however, reinforced by my snarling stomach, so I didn't answer his dawning smile.

"I beg your pardon," he said, somewhat grandiloquently, sweeping off his hat to show heavy yellow-brown hair so rough and thick that it resembled an animal's pelt. "I'm Colin McReynolds, foreman of Smoke Valley ranch. Mrs. Lindsay—" Was it my imagination,

11

or did his voice change at her name? "—Mrs. Lindsay got a bad headache on the way in. She saw me and asked if I'd fetch you—and I'm in a tear because it'll be getting dark and I need to see to a few things. It's not your fault. I'm sorry I was late."

His smile now was winning indeed, so that I sternly warned myself not to fall for any outdoorsy cigarette-ad type. There was no point, though, in nursing a grudge.

"I'm sorry to have created problems for you," I said as we moved toward the baggage area. "But I'm absolutely famished. Even a candy bar would help!" And I gazed about for a vending machine.

"We can do a little better than that," said Colin McReynolds, in one motion tipping the skycap who produced my plaid hanging bag and unmatching pullman, and hefting them himself without slackening his long stride. "I always have emergency food in the pickup. It pays in this country."

I almost ran to keep up with him as he swung out of the terminal and fairly loped for the parking lot. He tossed my luggage into the back of an olive-green pick-up and, again with that fluid continuation of one action into the next, opened the door on the passenger's side and boosted me into the cab.

"Sorry to hustle you," he said, producing a metal box from under the seat and handing it to me. "But that damned yak got into the flower beds again and—"

"Yak?" I echoed, casting him a fearful glance. Had I been abducted by a madman?"

"Yes, yak." For a moment he was engaged in maneuvering us out of the lot, but once we were on the road, he flicked me a side glance. "Open the box, Miss Redcoat. There's jerky and nut cakes and crackers, and a Thermos of coffee under your seat. By the way, what *is* your name? Shana—Mrs. Lindsay—was so upset she only told me to look for a girl in a red trenchcoat."

He sounded normal. Anyway, I'd heard it was best to humor the demented. "I'm Janet Richardson. Jan for short."

"I like that," he nodded. "A long name for solemn occasions and a short one for everyday."

I summoned up my courage. "Did you say *yak?*"

"Sure. Samson, we call him, because he's got all this hair hanging down to the ground."

"Does the ranch have a zoo or something?" I asked, chewing some jerky and feeling very frontierish.

"No, we just run Herefords. But I talked Britt—that's Mr. Lindsay—into importing a yak to mix with our stock. Yaks have some very handy tricks that I hope can be passed to cross-breed offspring. They dig down under snow to get to grass, their long coats are nice in severe freezes, and they're extremely self-reliant."

"Has the cross worked?"

"We've got some calves. We don't know yet if they'll reproduce, but if they do, and pass on the characteristics of Old Samson, then they'll be quite a breed of cattle."

"Cattle-yaks," I couldn't resist punning.

His head went back and he roared with laughter before casting me a reproachful look. "Ouch! I hope you don't do that very often."

"No, I'm usually accused of square solemnity."

"A sense of humor may help you at Smoke Valley," he said, watching the road more intently than he perhaps needed to, since it was only just beginning to climb and curve. "How did you hear about the job?"

*Careful,* I warned myself. *Careful, Jan. From now on, you can't blurt out answers without stopping to think.*

My heart lurched, chilled a bit, and, intensely aware of the man beside me, I thought that for all I knew *he* had been Lars Nordstrom—no, not unless Mrs. Lindsay was in on whatever had happened. She had vouched for Nordstrom's authentic existence.

If any summer staff were still around, it would be fairly easy to find out if Nordstrom really had been a frequent guest, get a description of him. Mother completely accepted Mrs. Lindsay's goodwill and veracity, but I was reserving judgment. I wasn't going to trust anyone at Smoke Valley, not for a long time anyway.

"A friend of mine worked at the lodge a few years ago, and she mentioned that someone stays through the winter," I said in a tone I hoped was casual and honest. "I was interested then, but of course I couldn't try for the job till I was through school."

"And now you are?"

"Last June."

"High school or college?" he asked, quite poker-faced.

"College," I returned haughtily. If he could ask questions, so could I. "Have you worked at the ranch very long?"

"Grew up here," he said.

"Oh. Your father worked at Smoke Valley, too?"

"You might say."

"And you've been foreman quite a while?"

He laughed. "Since I got out of school. I studied range management and animal husbandry."

"And played football, I suppose."

"No. I fenced and wrestled."

Curiouser and curiouser. "I fence," I said, more challengingly than I intended. "Maybe we can have a match someday."

He glanced at me, a smile tugging at his long straight mouth. "I'd have a big advantage in reach."

"Yes, but maybe you're out of practice," I said with a glint of malice, aware that we were already fencing—with words, trying to find the other's vulnerable points. "I was regional women's champion."

"Foil, saber, or épée?"

"Saber."

He gave me a look of real respect and keen appraisal. "So. You're a tiger, for all that defenseless-sweet-maid manner!"

"I'm not aggressive, Mr. McReynolds. But I won't be leaned on, either."

"Did you bring your mask and saber?"

"No. I certainly didn't expect to find a fencer up here!"

"I can probably outfit you." He chuckled. "Well, this

14

will be an unexpected pleasure. When I get mad at that damned yak, I can snowmobile over and challenge you!"

"Lots of luck," I tossed back. "The snow gets too bad for cars and trucks?"

He gave a long whistle. "You better believe it! Of course, the lodge and ranch are well stocked. We won't get hungry. But once winter closes down, you sure won't see town often."

"That's all right." I shrugged.

"Is it? Why, Miss Richardson?" He gave me a long, unsettling stare. "Why would any girl, much less a pretty one, hide away in an isolated lodge all winter?"

Fear gripped me. Supposing he *was* Nordstrom? Supposing he somehow suspected I was Anne's sister? The muscles of my throat were so tense that I had to swallow hard before I could answer.

"I'm not hiding. It's just that in between school and either more school or going to work, I'd like some quiet time to think, decide what I want to do, what my goals are ..."

He did chortle then, while I seethed with resentment. What I had said was true, though if it hadn't been for Anne's disappearance I probably would have considered a dropout season like this self-indulgence. I was resolved not to take any more money from Mother, and also determined to be well-established in my work, teaching remedial reading, before I even thought about getting married.

In spite of what I had told McReynolds, I *did* have a few general aims. I loved to read so much that I wanted to do what I could to help children who might otherwise miss that pleasure.

And I wanted to love some man someday, be loved by him, and have children. I would substitute-teach, or put in a few hours a day while they were little, and go back to full-time work when they started school.

I wanted, to sum it all up, the best of being both human and woman. For me, the definition of best needed a man. I hadn't met him yet. But someday maybe I would. And if I didn't—well, if I didn't, I'd teach! Maybe adopt children. I didn't want any shiftless charming Duprees in my life.

But Colin McReynolds was still chuckling in that soft, infuriating way. "Seems you've got quite a lot of soul-searching mapped out, Miss Richardson! If you work through it in one winter, you'll do very well." A strange note darkened his voice. "A hell of a lot better than most of us ever do."

"Don't you like your job?"

"The ranch?" He seemed to come back from a distance. "Wouldn't do anything else. But—there are different ways, styles, of doing the same thing. Of course," he added with what I took as condescension, "you're too young to have found that out."

"How do you know what I know?"

"Bless your bones, I don't!" he said, so genially that I couldn't stay affronted. "What I say is based on what I've learned, which is that many people never examine their lives or ends—and those who do often sit around like moulting chickens and only ponder the futility of it all. There's much of life you only get by taking a long deep breath and jumping in."

"I'll jump," I assured him. "But I want this winter first."

"Just so you don't keep it," he said slowly. "Even though you are the winter keeper."

The way he said it made my skin prickle. "What do you mean?"

"Hibernation is useful, even vital, during the cold. But it slows down the life processes till the creature is all but dead."

"I won't be hibernating!"

"Not physically, but . . ." He swept another glance from those penetrating storm-gray eyes that had long sun-bleached lashes and strong bleached eyebrows. "Miss Richardson, it's none of my business, but you don't strike me as a confused youngster who's headed for the hills to ponder her life's work. I think you're upset about something. Hurt. And at your age, again begging your pardon and indulgence, ma'am, that usually means a man."

I was upset and grieving still about Anne. It was certainly possible that I might behave like someone with a secret sorrow or gnawing pain. If McReynolds was suspicious, if he thought at all I might be connected with Anne, it would be just as well to let him think thwarted love accounted for any oddities in my behavior.

"Are you married, Mr. McReynolds?" I asked sweetly.

"Hunh-*uh!*"

"How old are you?"

"Twenty-eight."

"That," I thrust, "usually means trouble with women. Or a woman. Or maybe you hibernate all the time?"

His shoulders hunched forward for the slightest fraction of a second before he gave a dry little laugh. "Cagey little devil!" he growled. "You know, I'll bet you are pretty good with a saber. Okay. But I'll bet a year's pay you're here for more than soul-searching."

We turned off the highway, followed a narrow paved road for a while, and turned again, sharply, on a broad gravel one. A rustic sign with an arrow read SMOKE VALLEY LODGE . . . SMOKE VALLEY RANCH.

The last lap. My stomach knotted. I felt sick and scared. We were in tall pines and aspens now, gradually ascending. The aspens were brilliant yellow, breathtaking against the dark giant evergreens. Even in my apprehension, I strained to see all I could of incredible vistas, stretching sometimes past sparkling lakes, sometimes over valleys to mountains enveloped in a soft autumnal haze. We passed sheer stone cliffs and eroded statue-like formations, glimpsed a bear, saw what had to be a moose.

"There's a coyote," Colin McReynolds said, with veer of his chin. At first I only saw the golden autumn grass, high beside a stream, but then some hint of movement solidified the animal, gilded fur lit by late sun to the color of grass. His ears pricked forward and he pounced.

"Hunting mice," Colin explained, and I thought that

his hair, with the sun on it, would be the same shade as the coyote's.

We passed occasional floats of vapor, often low to the ground, sometimes curling high, which Colin told me were from hot springs. I saw goldenrod, brilliant red fireweed, and what looked like gooseberries. and Colin said that the trees with blue berries were junipers and that the splashes of orange on some of the huge rocks were algae, which also colored many of the fantastic formations in Yellowstone.

"Look!" I cried, as a small, sleek brown creature streaked across the rocks and bounded a good ten feet across to an opposite ledge. "What is that?" It was too little for a rabit and anyway, even in its flash of motion, I had seen that it had stubby ears. If it possessed a tail, it wasn't obvious.

"Pika, rock rabbit, cony, calling hare, slide rat," listed Colin, smiling as if he liked the creature. "You'll see a lot of them. They make hay and live off it all winter. *They*," he added with a mischievous side glance, "don't hibernate."

I ignored that, but it was getting chilly. The sun was behind the far mountains now, though its rays crimsoned the highest peaks to our right, those that were bare and above the timber. I turned up the collar of my trenchcoat, wished I had its lining zipped in, and wondered if Colin would make some annoying comment if I tucked my feet beneath me.

"Cold?" he asked. "Let me heat it up for a minute and then you can wrap that blanket behind us around you."

"Thanks," I said, turning to tug out the folded plaid blanket stored in the niche between seat and window.

I was snug in a few minutes. Warmth, excitement, and weariness combined to make me nearly doze off as dusk closed in and the surroundings softened and blurred.

Had Colin known Anne? I longed to ask, but couldn't think of a subtle way. And the Lindsays—what would they be like? And that child who had been so rude over the phone?

What would happen to me in Smoke Valley where I would be the winter keeper? Whatever Colin thought, I wasn't going to hibernate. If it were possible, I meant to learn what had happened to Anne, the truth about Nordstrom.

And I mustn't get sleepy like this around Colin McReynolds, let down my guard. It would be a contest all the way, even without sabers. The little pika ... the coyote whose thick hair was like Colin's ...

The next thing I knew, the pick-up jarred to a stop. "Here we are." I straightened at Colin's voice, yawned guiltily, and caught sight of a looming structure before he switched off the headlights.

"Over and out," he said briskly, already around to my side of the cab, practically hauling me out and setting me on my feet. "You'll forgive me if I drop you and run. Got to be sure Samson's out of trouble for at least the night."

He hauled my luggage out of the back, setting off for the building which had light glowing from several windows. The long broad verandah, railed with crossed peeled limbs, had a lamp lit above a huge rough door overspread by an immense set of antlers. As we climbed up a short flight of stone steps, Colin said, "Shana was going to send someone over with dinner. Tomorrow, Shana—Mrs. Lindsay—will come by or send for you."

He pushed open the door. The hall was so vast I blinked. It was the width of the whole building with stairways leading up to shadowy balconied overhangs reaching back to more of the second floor. The ceiling was so high, cathedral-arched above the main hall, that it was shrouded in darkness.

A fire burned in a big fireplace at the end of the hall. A wagon-wheel chandelier lit an area where couches and chairs were grouped casually. The rest of the hall was stacked with tables and chairs like a restaurant after hours.

"Hey!" shouted Colin. "Miss Richardson's here!"

His voice echoed, but there was no answer.

"Hell's bells," he said angrily. Striding across the hall, he went around a stone divider. "Probably Paula came and went so she wouldn't have to do anything extra. Let's see if there's some food. If there isn't, I'll drive you by the ranch and they can feed you and bring you back themselves, damn it, if they can't greet you properly!"

An open arch led into a big kitchen. The room was comfortable and filled with a tantalizing odor. A casserole showed through the glass door of one of the double ovens built in beside the biggest range top I'd ever seen. There were two giant freezers and three refrigerators. Colin opened the nearest one and made a sound of grudging approval.

"Well, you won't starve. I'll put your things in the cook's room just behind here. Will you be all right or shall I check back when I've seen to that yak?"

The expanse behind the kitchen was full of shadows, but if I meant to stay here all winter, it wouldn't do to give in to silly fits of imagination.

"I'll be fine," I said, much more calmly than I felt.

"Good girl," he approved, nudging open a door with his boot.

He was caught off balance by a swift lithe figure that almost knocked him backwards.

# 3

Colin McReynolds clamped the girl's arms down to her long flanks, giving her a shake. "Cecile, don't do that, damn it!"

She cast him a bright taunting smile, gazing past him to me. Her green eyes—wide, spaced far apart, accented by slim dark eyebrows—might have been a prowling cat's. except for the pupils which were human. Her flesh was a rich cream coffee, and she had pointed small breasts hugged by a tight-fitting knit shirt open deep to show a quick, rapid beat at the base of her slender throat. Except for her breasts, she could have been a thin, angular boy, except I doubted that any boy, even a gay one, ever had that slow provocative way of just parting rather broad lips to show beautiful, small teeth.

But the most stunning thing about her was what I can only describe as a long spun-gold Afro. A kinky nimbus framing her narrow face with its full pouty mouth, so that she could have been an angel playing truant from some clustered reverence above a Madonna's head to lie on a beach, soaking ripening sun into her fibers till she had the hue of light and earth.

Releasing her, warily taking a long step back, Colin said, "Miss Richardson, this is Cecile Lindsay. Cecile, this is Miss Richardson."

"I knew that," returned the high, unsexed voice I'd heard on the phone. "I brought over the food so I could see what she was like."

How old was she? Mature thirteen, immature seventeen? I really couldn't guess, she was so far from anything I had ever encountered. I couldn't, however, doubt the scorn in her tone or its possessive wheedling as she flicked those huge green eyes from me to the tall man, who looked edgy and annoyed.

"You've got to see about Samson, don't you, Colin? Take me with you."

"I'll drop you at the house," he said.

"No. I want to go with you." Gold hair shimmered as she thrust up her chin. "Please, Col. I'm not afraid of Samson."

"I am," he said flatly. "And you ought to be, you silly kid! Get your coat. I'm taking you home."

"Don't bother. I've got the jeep parked out back." She didn't move. Her eyes had strayed back to me.

Colin took a fringed leather jacket off an antlered hanger and held it in a way that made the girl shrug and slip into it. "Come on, Cecy," he commanded. "Miss Richardson has to unpack."

"I'd help her."

"Young lady, you're going home. Right now. Hop in that jeep and I'll follow you."

She moved toward the back of the lodge, shoulders hunched in mute anger. As she passed, she let her eyes slide coolly up and down me. Her face was impassive, but something in her manner radiated hostility that was physically withering.

Unbelievable. What could she have against me?

"Thanks for bringing the food," I told her. "Good night."

"Good night," she said, as if she grudged the words.

Colin looked at me for a second, as if he was about to tell me something, then nodded slightly and strode through the flickering shadows of the great front hall. Hand on the latch, he paused, gleams from the fireplace streaking that coyote hair.

"Bolt both doors," he said. "They've got automatic locks, but the bolts are good old-fashioned extra insurance." He touched a recess behind a mounted set of small antlers by the door. "The door keys are here," he said. "Better put one on your key chain."

He didn't say good-night, just closed the door firmly. I heard his boots on the broad verandah, opened my mouth to call thanks, and then realized he couldn't hear.

For some reason, before I locked the main door through which he had gone, I walked to the end of the corridor and shot the heavy iron bolt above the lock. A motor started close outside, then I heard the pick-up, and the sounds merged, rolling off together.

Passing through the entire length of the building, I bolted the front entrance, watching the fire streaming upwards behind the empty chairs.

Somehow a place that usually has lots of people in it seems haunted when they aren't there. I located a switch by the door and turned on the chandelier lights. These cheered the big hall, which must have been used for lounging, recreation, and dining. A creak came from the wings above. I stiffened, straining to hear, then laughed at my own nervousness.

A big frame structure like this with lots of upstairs rooms was going to make plenty of weird noises. I would have to get used to them.

Arriving at the lodge after dark was intimidating enough, but Cecile Lindsay had troubled me, made me acutely uneasy. She must be the Lindsay's daughter. For all her youth, she obviously wanted Colin McReynolds—perhaps had him, for all I knew, though his forbidding attitude with her would appear to rule out the existence, yet, of any physical relationship. I didn't see how he could help being tempted. Did the Lindsays know how the child behaved?

I moved toward the kitchen, tantalized by the casserole's delicious smell. A hot meal before I unpacked would soothe me down, give me a better outlook, steady my tense nerves. At least, thank goodness, I wasn't living in the ranch house with Cecile!

Had she known Anne?

Whatever else I might think about the Lindsays' reception of me, dinner was exactly what I needed after a long day of traveling with almost no food. The orange porcelain baking dish held wild rice, mushrooms, and chicken cooked in perfect amounts of wine, sour cream, and herbs. There were celery and carrot sticks in the refrigerator, a container of blanc mange, a bowl of seedless grapes, and on the long heavy table that sat in the middle of the kitchen were a loaf of homemade rye bread, what looked like home-churned butter, a bowl of fruit, a crock of cookies, and a beautifully golden-crusted pie with clear juices of cherry thickened around sugared slits.

The refrigerator was also well-stocked with cheeses, spreads, salad things, juices, soft drinks, and milk.

Pulling a stool up to the table, I had a glass of milk, two helpings of the potent chicken-rice, a slice of buttered bread, and, with a tardy effort at control, only a sliver of the succulent pie.

The kitchen was good, with its high, whitewashed beamed ceiling, cedar walls and cabinets, and a window that ran the length of the room so that in daytime there must be wonderful natural light beaming off the polished red tile floor. There were rows of utensils, pans, and lids hanging at eye level above the working space near the stove-oven complex. A glazed white tile patterned with animals and birds covered all the counters, and all the walls between counters and cabinets. A larger row of this pattern bordered the wall just below the ceiling. There was no attempt at coordination, but the functional, accessible way everything was arranged, coupled with plenty of space and gleaming tile, made it a happy room, right for its purpose.

Reassured by the kitchen and the comforting meal, I

went into the room behind it where Colin had hung my fold-up bag and set the other case on a low chest beneath a window.

Parting the curtains I looked out. For a moment, there was only blackness.

Unreasoning alarm gripped me. It seemed I *must* glimpse something out there—something to prove I wasn't completely isolated, locked up at night in the place from which my sister had disappeared so strangely. I *had* to see, catch at least a glimmer from the window.

I cupped my hands on either side of my eyes, shielding out the room. Slowly I could see sparkles in the sky, high stars. I always loved to watch them, especially in the country where city lights didn't interfere. And then a glow from earth level flared suddenly, as if someone had turned on a lamp. I couldn't guess how far away it was, only that it was distant. But the constant steady shine eased my irrational dread. I dropped the lined monk's-cloth drapes, turned, and surveyed the room I was going to live in that winter.

Smoke Valley Lodge's cook had very nice quarters, I decided, glancing from the big bed with its brass-knobbed posts and scarlet wool coverlet to a large oak dresser topped by a double mirror. Again, the floor was polished red Spanish tile, softened by several Indian blankets. There was a desk in one corner with shelves reaching from it to the ceiling, a chair, and a black leather recliner opposite a small TV on rollers.

The personal things that give a room character were gone, but the wall above the bed was covered with expertly arranged water colors in matched thin black frames. The pictures showed animals and birds in individualistic poses: pika, deer, bighorn sheep, moose, bear, wolf, coyote, several kinds of squirrel, a swan, geese, ducks, and birds I didn't know. They were done with such skill and understanding that I stood on tiptoe to make out the initials slurred in the corner of the pika's rockslide. CM.

Colin McReynolds? I dismissed the notion. There

must be millions of people with CM for initials. I opened my suitcase and began to distribute its contents into the drawers of the chest. I had been wondering idly if the cook was a man or woman, and the drawer lining seemed to clear up the small mystery. What man would have his chest lined with quilted satin splashed with roses?

The only books left on the shelves were a dictionary and world atlas. Before the snows closed in, I'd better try to get a supply of books. Crewel work, too, maybe, and macrame. I had a feeling I was going to have a lot of long lonely hours in this lodge during the next seven months, and I wasn't that keen about television.

There was a long closet with plenty of storage space. I hadn't brought many hang-up clothes, depending mostly on pants and sweaters, so it didn't take long to arrange what belonged in the closet and shut the folding cedar door.

The bathroom was small, white, bright, and blue. I didn't mind its lack of a bathtub since I'm a shower-lover. There was a thick shaggy blue all-over rug that I knew would be appreciated as winter deepened. An ample stack of towels and washcloths filled a chrome shelf-rack, and the mirrored medicine cabinet was outsize, so that there was a shelf left over after the most generous spreading out of my toiletries.

And so to bed?

I glanced at my watch, remembering I had jumped a time zone. My watch said ten o'clock, but it was really eleven. I was physically tired, but my mind was restless, spinning from one face to another, from one person's riddle to another's.

Anne: her eyes laughed at me before I had a flash of her vanishing beneath foaming waves, mouth open in a strangling cry. That image faded to the dreadful moment in the morgue when I'd had to view her broken, sea-marred body. When I shoved that horror away, I confronted the jeering green gaze of that beautiful wanton child, Cecile.

Colin McReynold's craggy features closed over hers. His look was inscrutable, but his mouth, it seemed, could bend to either cruelty or kindness.

And there were the faces I hadn't seen. Shana Lindsay's; her husband's, that of Lars Nordstrom, people who worked at the ranch. And the cook who made that superlative dinner.

Mother hadn't asked me to phone on arrival, but after what had happened to Anne, she was probably anxious about me. There was no phone in the cook's room, but I had noticed a wall-type in the kitchen.

I put on some milk to heat for chocolate, poured syrup into a large mug, perched by the stove, and dialed station-to-station.

At the third ring, Mother's soft voice came over the line. "Hello, darling," I said, pouring the heated milk into the syrup and giving it a stir. "I'm all set to turn in, but thought I'd let you know I got here all right."

"I'm glad you did, Jan," said Mother. "I suppose it's too early for—for you to have learned anything?"

"I haven't met the Lindsays yet, their foreman met me. I can't ask direct questions about Anne without rousing suspicions, and though everyone here may be perfectly honest, we can't just assume that."

"Mrs. Lindsay sounded terribly nice and concerned."

"Let's hope she is. But I'm going to play it very cool."

I told her about the lodge, gorgeous Cecile, the cunning little pika, my comfortable room. I didn't tell her how spooky the shadowy, creaking place appeared on first experience, or how isolated I felt even though I was only a few miles from the ranch, but some of the atmosphere must have got through my words or tone.

"I wish you weren't alone in that big old place," mother said. "This foreman—do you think he might stop by often to see how you are?"

"I certainly won't ask him," I said drily. "But I'm sure the ranch will keep in touch, and I do have a phone. Probably I'm worlds safer here than in St. Louis or at college."

Our St. Louis apartment had been broken into twice in the past three years by thieves who had grabbed portable, easy-to-sell things like the small TV, record player, typewriter, and radio. And my room at school! I hated to think of the books, record albums, hair dryers, and clothes that had been "borrowed" or simply taken.

"That's possibly true," said Mother. "But if I don't hear from you every week by phone or mail, I'm going to be right on the line to Mrs. Lindsay!"

"Don't worry, dear, I'll be in touch one way or the other." Actually I wasn't that bad a correspondent. Anne was the one who disappeared in whatever she was doing. I was a post-carder, true, but a reliable one. Giving Mother the kitchen phone number, I said goodnight, hung up, settled back with my remaining chocolate, and froze.

Someone was walking through the lodge.

But I had bolted the doors!

For a moment I was paralyzed; the steps were very close. I snatched up the phone, looked desperately around for a book, an emergency number, realizing in icy lucidity that it was a long way to any police. The ranch number ... if I only knew it! O for Operator seemed my only chance. Even if I was attacked before I could say anything, the operator might be able to hear commotion, trace the call.

I dialed O, put the phone out of sight behind the cookie crock, took a long, sharp knife from the magnetic rack above the stove, and held it behind me as I faced the door.

The footsteps paused.

I heard the tinny, distant voice over the phone saying, "Operator—this is the operator! Can I help you?"

"Miss Richardson?" came a man's voice from outside. "Miss Richardson, this is Britt Lindsay. May I come in?"

A criminally intentioned person wouldn't bother with introductions. I hung up the phone with a muttered apology, put the knife down but left it within reach, and said in a rather wobbly tone, "Did you knock? I thought I'd locked the doors."

"You had, the principal ones," said the man who appeared in the doorway, and stopped there as if to demonstrate the impeccability of his intentions. "I knocked, but you didn't hear me, and I thought something might be wrong."

I might have been asleep, too. The thought of someone being able to come in at will frightened me, even though the man must have some excuse for his behavior and didn't seem threatening. He smiled at me in an apologetic way.

"It must seem rather abrupt all round, Miss Richardson—Shana's not being able to meet you, Colin being in a rush because of that incorrigible flower-loving yak. If Shana had developed her—her headache before she left the main ranch, someone else could have fetched you. As it was, only Colin was near enough not to keep you waiting long. I was distressed about what you must think of us."

And he stood in the doorway, still with that tentative, almost shy smile. He had the fairest hair I had ever seen on anyone but platinum blondes. At first I had thought it was white, but it had a hint of rich honey to it. His eyes, too, were startling, a very pale amber.

Surprisingly, his complexion was not that of an outdoorsman, though he wore khaki stockman's pants and a sheepskin jacket over a plaid shirt. His accent was unusual—almost British, I thought—and his diffident behavior couldn't have been in greater contrast to Colin McReynold's blunt, head-on tactics.

*Why,* I thought, getting angry in retrospect at the way he had practically abducted me from the phone booth, *Colin treated me as a nuisance—a—a yak in a flower bed because I interfered with his work! It wasn't my fault!*

It was Colin who had told me to lock the doors. Yet Britt Lindsay had found a way in. And that troubled me, whatever his excuses.

"I've been made most comfortable," I told him.

"There was a wonderful dinner, and of course I do understand that emergencies happen and people are busy. Mr. McReynolds thought your wife would come by or send for me in the morning."

"That's actually why I've come," said Lindsay. He lifted his silvery eyebrows inquiringly. "Would you mind if I had a cup of coffee?"

"Do have a seat," I invited, turning toward the sink. "Is instant all right?"

"Fine. But," he laughed boyishly, "I hope there's cream."

"There is," I assured him, putting on a teakettle and finding cups and saucers in the first cupboard I opened. I already knew where spoons and sugar were, so it took only a few minutes to be sitting opposite him as we sipped our coffee.

"I'm glad you're settled in well," said Smoke Valley's owner. "Have you been in this part of the country before?"

"No. But what I saw before it got dark looks beautiful."

"It is. We'll have to see that you get to journey around a bit before the snows bog us down and change the scenery."

"It must be splendid when snow covers the mountains and woods."

He nodded. "Yes, but it can also be deadly. Now we can get around on snowmobiles to tend the stock or run necessary journeys, and that's helped a lot." His eyes went slowly, lingeringly over my face. "Are you used to severe winters, Miss Richardson?"

"Not compared to what I'm sure you get here."

"Do you like winter sports?"

"I've never tried any, outside of sledding when I was a little girl, throwing snowballs, and seeing if I could make a bigger snow queen than my sister."

Sister? I almost bit my lip. It didn't really matter, almost everyone had a sister, but I must be on guard never to let any betraying detail slip.

"If you don't know the region, don't have a passion for skiing and such, what brought you here?" Britt Lindsay's manner had changed suddenly, as swiftly as a hawk's glide might plunge into a swooping dive.

<h1 style="text-align:center">4</h1>

Totally unprepared for the question, I pretended to savor my coffee, hoping he couldn't detect the increased rapidity of my heartbeat. "I wasn't quite ready to go to work and was pretty tired of school," I said, in what I prayed was a suitably casual way. "It seemed that a remote area where there'd be plenty of time to think was just what I needed."

A smile glimmered on his well-shaped mouth. "A retreat from the world?"

"No. A chance to contemplate it. Think about my life instead of just *doing*."

"But surely you could find a spiritual haven nearer home."

I shrugged. "Part of the whole sorting out process, for me, was to get into completely new surroundings. When I heard about this job, it sounded perfect."

Those light eyes swept over me again before he smiled, charmingly, and rose to his feet. He was perhaps even taller than Colin, but he was slender, almost delicate in build.

"I certainly hope your season here fulfills all your needs and hopes, Miss Richardson. Our winter keepers have usually been schoolteachers driven bonkers by their pupils, divorcees licking their wounds, ski or tobaggan fiends, and on one occasion, a naturalist who was writing a book on the Yellowstone area." He inclined his graceful head. "May I say that you offer a refreshing change?"

"That's nice of you."

"Candid." He hesitated long enough to make me grow edgy, hoping fervently that he wasn't the sort of clod who would try to finger me. He didn't seem that kind—he had been meticulously courteous—but he *had* walked in.

That memory jarred me. "Mr. Lindsay, before you go would you show me the door you came in through? I really do want to know where all the entrances and exits are."

"Of course you must," he agreed. "Come along."

He stood aside to let me pass, flicking on a powerful flashlight as we entered the main hall where the fire had sunk to fitful embers, erupting into flame now and then when a charred piece snapped. He switched on wall sconces that lit the rustic stairway to the balcony.

"To the top and straight back," he directed.

The balcony had benches and tables scattered around so that people could sit up here and see what was going on in the main hall. The waist-high railing was of peeled limbs lashed together with rawhide, their twisted spikes silhouetted eerily on the wall, resembling the horns of some giant animal.

The passageway before me was densely black. Britt Lindsay played his light along it and then turned on fluorescent bulbs sheathed in inverted angle beams to cast a soft diffuse glow along the hall. There were doors on either side.

"There are forty rooms up here," Britt explained. "Twenty on this side, twenty down the passageway reached by the other staircase. There's an exit at the end of each corridor, with a fire escape. They were locked but not bolted. We can bolt them now if it'd make you feel more secure." He laughed lightly. "If you aren't seen or heard of for a while, we can always break a window to get in and rescue you."

I felt like retorting that it was scarcely security-making to point out that bolts and locks by no means secured the lodge. Had his remark, reassuringly phrased, been intended to hint at my vulnerability?

"Let's hope no rescues are necessary," I said in a cool tone. Preceding him, I tested the door, found it locked, and shoved the bolt in place. Next we moved along the balcony to the other wing and bolted that door, too.

"That does it," said my employer briskly. "All approaches safe except the chimney."

"Thank you," I said, glancing back at the empty wings with their silent rooms. "It's been exceedingly kind of you."

"Oh, my pleasure." He bowed his head in that just slightly quaint, slightly old-fashioned style.

I saw him to the main door, keeping what I considered a safe but not remarkable distance from him.

"Good night," he said. "Will you come to the house for tea in the morning? Shana's eager to meet you."

"I'd enjoy that," I said. "Which way is it?"

"Oh, we'll send someone for you," Lindsay promised. "About ten?"

"Fine. I'll be ready."

He went out then, and though he wore boots, his tread was so soft that only the creaking planks betrayed his going.

I bolted the huge front door and went back to my room, thoroughly roused by the coffee and the unsettling effect of his unexpected late visit. Why had he asked those sudden sharp questions about my taking the job?

Had *he* known Anne? As a person, not temporary summer help?

I took a leisurely, soothing shower, as hot as I could enjoy, letting the water stream over me till the worst tensions and apprehensions eased. Drowsy languor crept through me with renewed effect more potent for having been held off so long. Within a few minutes of snuggling under the blankets of the big comfortable bed, I sank into heavy slumber.

When I awoke, soft hazy light blurred my surroundings. I yawned, stretched luxuriously, and curled up more into the pillows before I suddenly realized that these weren't my familiar thin ones, and that the bed was slightly softer than what I was used to.

I was in Smoke Valley Lodge! Really there, not just planning to be.

I sat up and swung out of bed in one motion, then ran to the window and pulled the drapes. Light flooded in, brilliant sunshine. Tall pines rose beyond the clearing around the lodge. Beyond them, peaking jaggedly into the dazzling blue sky, stretched mountains purpled by ground haze, the heat of the sun wooing the cold of the night.

I couldn't see the place from where last evening's comforting glow had come. It must be hidden by the forest. Nor could I see any other buildings. Pushing up the window, I caught a long tingling breath of the clear chill air, waking up from the bottom of my toes to the top of my head. I closed the window and dressed in a hurry because the room was nippy now, even after I turned on the electric heater.

It was nine o'clock. Someone would come for me at ten. I made toast from the homemade bread, brewed coffee, and made a swift reconnoiter of the lodge in daylight.

The balcony wasn't spooky now, but the closed rows of doors opening off the upstairs corridors did bother me a little. Trying to dispel this uneasiness, I went into several of the rooms.

There I saw bare-mattressed beds, desk-dressers with straight chairs perched atop, various kinds of easy chairs, portable TVs in a few rooms. Stripped-down lodgings waiting for occupants. Nothing either reassuring or alarming.

The big hall downstairs with its high vaulted rafters

made me feel tiny, an intruder, though sunlight spangled the tiles and cast bright patterns where it struck a surface. I didn't think I'd spend much time there. The kitchen-bedroom complex was comfortable and more to human scale, though I imagined wistfully what fun must go on in the main room when the lodge was full.

Anne had written about the sings at night, impromptu talent shows, when help mingled with guests. Had she met Lars Nordstrom at such a frolic, in this very hall?

Where was Nordstrom, that mysterious man of whom we could find no trace? Did the Lindsays know anything they weren't telling?

If Nordstrom was an assumed identity, as seemed very likely, the imposter could have deceived the Lindsays too, even over a period of several years. They might be completely honest, and probably were. It was even possible that Anne had died while on an escapade with Nordstrom, but I didn't believe it.

A deliberate lie to Mother and me while on a fling? No, it wasn't like her.

I retreated to my room, brushed my hair till it framed my face in a heavy straight fall of near-black, and brightened my mouth with lipstick. I had enough tan not to need other makeup, but I did tip my fingers with lotion and shape my eyebrows into more of an arch. They had a disconcerting tendency to stretch straight above my eyes, and though I didn't mind their being heavy, I did wish they had a more piquant shape. Anne's eyebrows had fanned into surprised wings; she always seemed to be asking an eager, delighted question.

Anne. The pain of loss—the anger at such waste— came washing over me. I held my breath till it ebbed enough to let me think.

Of the people who would have known her at least slightly, I had already met Cecile, Colin McReynolds, and Britt Lindsay. In a little while now I would be able to form some impression of Shana Lindsay. Since she had known Nordstrom and had said Anne was neglecting her work for him, it would seem that Shana was the most likely person to know if there were more to Anne's disappearance than had been admitted.

I was nervous, very edgy. It was almost ten. When I caught myself pacing the floor, I slung my purse over my shoulder and went out on the verandah.

Sheer marvel drove out my fears and tensions. From the long porch, I could see in a wide sweep from west to south to east. There were mountains everywhere, some distant, some marching in lower peaks with higher ones beyond, melting into the burning blue sky. To the west several billowing white funnels looked like earthbound clouds; south, there rose a terraced mesa, predominantly white but layered with white, pink, yellow, and yellow-green.

I walked toward it, since I'd be seen clearly there by whoever came for me. The sculptured terrace seemed to have been eaten out of the side of the mountain to which it was still attached at the back. Water dripped from above, running down the formation, here and there standing in shallow pools.

As I got closer, I could see that the crenellations were mineralized and hard, rather as if colored salt had been allowed to congeal along pinnacles and basins that dipped from level to level like an ultramodern fountain.

The strange fortress was moated from approach from the lodge by a narrow stream that apparently was fed by the drip of springs from the mountain. A rustic bridge of two broad logs, smoothed on one side and guarded by a handrail, led over the water, and rude steps had been made in the side of the cliff so that one could ascend just opposite the colored formation and admire it without endangering it.

I stood on the bridge, wishing I could cross but afraid of missing my escort. It *was* ten. Sighing, I turned, and as if to reward my decision, a jeep churned into the clearing in front of the lodge. A man jumped out and ran up the stairs of the lodge.

"I'm over here," I shouted, waving, but he seemed not

to hear me. So I hurried across the grounds and reached the jeep as my caller had given up banging on the door. He swung around, bandy-legged, to shield his eyes and peer about.

I waved again, and called, "Here I am!"

The man dropped his hand and faraway gaze, blinked, and focused on me. He was brown and wizened, thin gray hair showing under a hat that was so old and weathered that it was impossible to guess whether it had originally been blue or gray. He wore gold-rimmed spectacles, and he looked quite a lot like Harry Truman—that is, he had the same bulldog mouth set in tenacious good humor.

When he saw me, he took off the battered felt hat and nodded his head. "You be Miss Richardson?"

He spoke so loudly that I thought he must be rather deaf, and I answered as clearly as I could. "Yes. You must be from the ranch."

"That's right, ma'am. I'm Tam Cannon. Ready?"

"Yes, thank you."

"Don't be thanking me till you see what you're into," he grunted, opening the jeep door and giving me a hand up, though I felt that in view of his age it really ought to be the other way around.

He climbed into the driver's seat and we bumped along the main road till we reached the trees to the east where the road forked.

Tam stopped. "See anything coming?" he asked.

"No," I returned, my stomach tightening up. If he couldn't see ...

"What say?" he roared. "Don't mumble, lady! Young people anymore, all they do is mumble."

"No!" I yelled back at him. "The road's clear!"

He swung left. "Other way's the road to Billings," he said. "Ain't been there in a coon's age. Place has got plumb confusing. I liked it better afore the country got overrun with these durned cars and airyplanes!"

"But you drive a jeep," I shouted.

"Yup." He was gunning along so that we hit every dip in the road; I didn't see how riding a bucking horse could be much different, except that I'd have gotten mercifully ditched right away. He gave me a flash of pearly teeth which had to be artificial. "Now I don't mind a jeep, ma'am. It's like a work animal, nothin' shiny or high-falutin'. This'n is Betsy Second, named after my old roping horse. Betsy First and me still go for a canter pretty often, but she's earned her oats and pasture."

Tam Cannon looked to me as if he had earned retirement, too, but even on this brief acquaintance, I couldn't picture him doing nothing.

"Have you worked at Smoke Valley long?" I asked.

"Born here," he said, with a sweeping gesture. "My daddy worked for the first Lindsay, the one who started the ranch, back in 1878. Lindsay was from England, one of them remittance men, you know, son of some big lord. His older brother became Earl Somebody-or-other. Came over a couple of times to hunt. Couldn't hardly understand a word he said, but he was a good shot and fine rider."

"What's a remittance man, Mr. Cannon?"

"Well, some of those rich English families had wild sons or just lads who needed elbow room. Quite a lot of them came out West and their families bankrolled 'em." The old man chuckled. "Damn funny thing happened, ma'am! The first Lindsay's brother died, and so Lindsay was the Earl, like it or not. He went back and tried it for a year, but he just couldn't stand that quiet green civilized country after all this out here. So he chucked the title onto *his* younger brother and came back."

"Do the families still visit?"

"Well, Britt went to school in England." Tam Cannon spoke drily, as if he didn't altogether approve of the result. That explained Britt's slight accent, of course. "And every now and then a herd of the English Lindsays and their friends come over for the summer. Nice folks, mostly, just foreign. Colin, now, he was brought up on the ranch." A warm note entered Cannon's voice at the name.

"He's the foreman," I said. "He met me at the airport."

"He is the foreman," agreed the old cowboy. "But he's also a Lindsay on his mother's side. She was sister to Britt's daddy."

"Then—it looks as if Colin would be part owner of the ranch," I suggested.

"By rights he should be, especially since he keeps it going."

Cannon lapsed into brooding silence. I thought I'd better not probe, though questions swarmed in my mind. Colin hadn't hinted in any way that he was more than a hired man at Smoke Valley. But if he had a claim through his mother, surely he must feel some pride of ownership, some right in determining what went on.

We wheeled past a log cabin, and glancing through the trees beyond it, I could just make out a glimpse of the lodge. "This is Colin's place," Tam explained.

I was sure that the light that had comforted me last night came from this building. And I *thought* I was glad to know that Colin McReynolds was not far away, comparatively. Montana was already getting to me. Anything under twenty miles seemed fairly close!

I asked Tam Cannon the names of trees as we drove along. At first there were mostly lodgepole pine, growing tall and straight without much root, so that here and there we passed a few that had apparently blown down. As the road climbed, Cannon pointed out Englemann spruce, Douglas Fir, whitebark pine, limber pine, Rocky Mountain juniper, and aspen, absolutely breathtaking against the darker foliage with its sun-filtered yellow leaves and white trunks.

Along one vast rockslide, I saw piles of grass and plants, and a pika sat there washing its face like a small cat. I squealed with delight.

"Eh?" said Cannon.

"It was a pika," I said. "A rock rabbit."

He grinned. "See their hay? My eyes ain't so good."

40

"There are several heaps of grass and things."

Tam nodded. "They're letting it cure. Before long they'll move it into their dens and eat out of it all winter. Cute little fellers." He scowled and added for no reason that I could think of, "Dang shame some folks can't just enjoy God's critters instead of making all kinds of fuss and studies and experiments with 'em. I like to hunt, ma'am, and I ain't fixin' to give up my steaks, but there's some doin's I just can't stomach!"

I decided he was talking about laboratory experiments using animals, but there was no time to ask now because we were driving through a steel gate mounted to granite pillars from which a zigzag log fence stretched out to encircle several acres of grassy tableland lying at the bottom of rearing forested mountains.

The house—mansion, really—that sat in the middle of the park astonished me. I blinked and looked again, but it was still there.

Sparkling white, a two-storied frame house, it resembled, with its high columns, some of the old plantation houses I had seen on vacation in Maryland. Trees grew in strategic places around it, like selected specimens, and formal gardens were laid out on all sides of the house. If the yak had gotten into those, I could imagine the furor.

Of its style, the house was gracious and beautiful. But it looked strange, completely out of place with the jagged peaks thrusting into the bright blue beyond it. A house like that needed gentle slopes, soft rounded country.

"The first Lindsay's son built this house," snorted old Tam, wheeling up the broad graveled drive at a reckless speed that made me clutch the seat. "He always wished he could have been the English Earl, I reckon, sendin' Britt to school over there and all, tearing down a perfectly good log house and puttin' up this dang thing . . .'"

Still muttering, he choked the jeep to a halt, jumped down with amazing agility, and came around to help me descend. He looked me in the eye. We were the same height, even with his cowboy boots jacking him up several inches. He shook his head and gave a sigh.

"Well, go along to the house, ma'am. Mrs. Lindsay will want to see how you grip your teacup and speak your piece. Can't say I hold with havin' a young female over at the lodge all winter by herself—you sure wouldn't be there if you were my daughter." In spite of his disapproving words, there was an undercurrent of sympathy in his tone, and for just a minute, his gnarled old hand brushed my arm. "Now if you have any problems, little lady, you tell Colin or get word to me. Good luck."

He tipped his indeterminately-colored hat, mounted Betsy Second, and screeched off, while I advanced on the colonnaded mansion.

# 5

The big double doors had arched, sectioned windows at the very top, too high for anyone to see through. The brass knocker in front of me was shaped like a lion's head, its mouth open in threat. I banged it several times against the brass mount and waited, my mouth feeling terribly dry.

Meeting Shana Lindsay was my real test. And she was most likely to know the truth about Anne, have the secret of Nordstrom's identity.

Was she a nice woman, as Mother believed, or was she involved in Anne's disappearance? As I heard steps approaching the door, I realized that my hands were clenched, the palms wet. It took real effort to make my fingers relax and prepare a smile.

This froze as the door swung open wide and I stared into scornful green eyes in a creamy gold-brown face. Cecile was wearing a tentlike robe of embroidered natural muslin this morning. In spite of the chill, her slender, high-arched feet were bare, the nails painted frosty plum to match her fingertips, the elegant effect of which was spoiled by black rims showing where the polish was chipped.

The vibrant mass of tight-curled golden hair gave her the look of an angel, but her pouting mouth said she was determined to fall and take what she could with her.

"Oh, it's you," she said, managing to convey disgust.

"You were expecting Mick Jagger?" I asked, stepping inside.

If this girl chose not to like me, I was sorry for that, but I did not intend to try to placate or cajole the little witch. She messed with me and she'd get as good as she gave.

"Cecile," fluted a silvery voice. "Is that Miss Richardson? Please bring her back."

The child hitched a shoulder at me and led the way through a hall that could have been in a fine arts museum. A chest carved with flowers and vines intertwining the date 1610 sat under a long mirror in a gold baroque frame which gave back images of the portraits on the opposite wall above a velvet-cushioned settee.

These portraits must have been from England. Ladies showing much white bosom, a handsome man resembling Britt in a gorgeous uniform, a family grouping featuring several lapdogs, and several paintings of red-jacketed men in white breeches and black boots astride horses. In one picture they were gathering for the hunt, and in the other the chase was in full cry.

"The unspeakable in full pursuit of the uneatable," Oscar Wilde had dubbed fox-hunting. I was inclined to agree.

The hall ended with a closed-in staircase. On that wall hung one portrait only, which lacked the antique appearance of the others.

It showed a young girl in hunting clothes, a girl about the age of Cecile, but with an expression on her face as if she had just confronted an incredible horror. In one limp, graceful hand lay the thick red brush of a fox.

A thoroughly disturbing picture, but I had no time to pause to try to understand why. Cecile was already halfway inside an open door, looking back toward me impatiently. I gulped down a deep breath and stepped through the entrance.

I looked into the same eyes as the girl in the portrait, eyes set in an older face surrounded by hair as golden as Cecile's but straight and long, swept back with a cord of pearls.

I felt a moment of sheer wonder, followed by a keen awareness of my gangly height, my tomboy looks. Mother was pretty, and Anne had been lovely in a young fresh way, but this woman before me was so beautiful it hurt. She had a touch of the fey, perhaps, a remnant of whatever had illuminated her young features in the portrait with the pitiless flare of horror.

She had blue eyes, flawless honey skin, sculptured bones. She wore a turquoise velvet hostess gown scrolled with pearls, and matching high-heeled slippers.

"Miss Richardson?" She greeted me in a clear, singing voice, extending manicured fingers which definitely did not have dirt beneath the nails, and which made me hotly conscious of my own close-trimmed, somewhat ragged ones. "So sorry I couldn't meet you yesterday, my dear. I'm Shana Lindsay. You've met Cecile, I think?"

"She brought over my dinner," I said, smiling at the girl, who only regarded me with hostile sulkiness before she turned abruptly and left the room.

Stupid to let a moody child make me feel so rejected, but she could. I swallowed and produced another smile for my employer. "The food was delicious, and my room is most pleasant."

"Splendid," said Mrs. Lindsay, arranging herself on a peacock brocade loveseat. "Do sit down. May I call you Jan?"

"Please," I said gratefully. "What a magnificent home you have, Mrs. Lindsay. You must love it."

She cast me a sharp glance, shrugged, then smiled "It *is* magnificent, but frankly, I'd prefer glass and steel in a New York penthouse, or rattan in the Bermudas. Most of the furnishings are from England and were here when Britt and I married. The trouble with heirlooms is that you can't get rid of them, and they defy—at least in such numbers—any attempt at individuality."

She, like Britt, had an almost-accent, a polished, delightful intonation. She picked up a silver bell and tinkled it. "What will you have, Jan? Tea or coffee? Orange juice?"

"Whatever you're having, please."

"Since I was brought up in England, I'm addicted to tea." She laughed in a way that echoed the pure sound of the bell. "But don't be meek, dear. Ask for what you want."

"Tea seems the thing to have in this room," I said, trying without obvious staring to take in all that I could.

I was sitting on a couch done in gold velvet, and what I vaguely suspected was a Regency table stood between us, four golden lion heads topping the legs, while gilt scrolling ran around the inlaid sides. The fireplace was built high with alabaster figures: Diana, the huntress, on one side, a handsome young man on the other, and a stag and hounds in between them. These sculptures were almost life-size and reached nearly to the top of the ceiling.

Oriental rugs were scattered on the polished wood floor. Two bow windows looked out over flower beds, mostly cleaned and tidied for winter. Book cabinets with small-paned glass doors ran along one entire side of the room, and a polished trestle table and heavily carved chairs were near it. At the other end of the room was another grouping of antique chairs and two sofas, interspersed with lovingly polished tables. A writing desk, its carved top folded up to hide pigeonholes, occupied a well-lit space, and a grand piano was just behind Mrs. Lindsay.

There were more paintings, the largest one depicting a castle, gray stone, rectangular, with a flag flying from one tower. Beneath it was a large, very old map of the County of Hampshire, England, and I was sure that the castle was the ancestral Lindsay home and that it must be in Hampshire.

A tall, handsome brown woman entered, black hair coiled in thick braids at the nape of her neck in a way that cast her strong features into relief. She was not young, but she had an ageless, dignified beauty.

"Paula," Mrs. Lindsay said, without glancing up, "We'll have tea, please."

"Yes, madam. Will Mr. Lindsay join you?"

"No, he's busy. Jan, this is Paula. Paula, this is Jan Richardson, the winter keeper."

The Indian woman let her gaze rest on me an instant, nodded, and then moved away, silent and graceful as a deer. She wore moccasins beneath a long black skirt, silver bracelets, and a purple velveteen blouse.

"Will you be afraid at the lodge?" Mrs. Lindsay asked.

"A little, perhaps, but I'd expect to get over that."

The blue eyes dwelled on me till I felt uneasy. "A sensible attitude," she said at last, taking an aromatic cigarette from the engraved silver box on the table and offering me one. "Not all young women are so realistic. They think they'll love winter sports and flirting with forest rangers and cowboys. We've only had two women who lasted the whole season, one a writer and the other a divorcee."

"Would it be easier to hire a man?"

"Oh, we could find plenty of them who wouldn't be afraid, but they haven't proved much good at keeping the lodge in order and the kitchen operable. On the whole, we've found it better to have a woman, since it's no problem to send one of our men over to knock snow off the roof when the load gets heavy enough to threaten it, or do any other maintenance that's too hard for a girl." She brought her head up suddenly, piercing me with those deep blue eyes so that I felt as if she'd touched me physically. "Why did you take this job, Jan?"

*Anne ... Anne, my little sister, supposed to be drowned, supposed to have gone off with this Lars Nordstrom you vouch for ...*

For a sickening, frightening moment, I felt as if Shana

Lindsay were reading my mind, but I controlled my breathing, producing a smile and what I hoped was a casually surprised answer.

"I thought I'd told you that, Mrs. Lindsay. I didn't feel like either going back to school for my master's or jumping right into teaching. I wanted time and a place to think, reach some conclusions about how to build my life."

She shook her gleaming head as Paula brought in the tea, set it down, and glided out. "You seem a terrifyingly sane young person. When I was your age I never thought from one day to the next about what was going to happen."

"That sounds as if it could be fun."

She gave me another long look. "Not," she said drily, "when you get to the end of some of the consequences. But sufficient to the day! Do you take milk and sugar?"

"Yes, please."

She poured the tea into white cups with gold rims, adding a lump of sugar to each cup with silver tongs, then poured the milk. I thanked her and took one of the nut-crusted little rolls she offered from a matching plate.

Briskly and precisely, she outlined my tasks. I was to see that water was kept at a dribble during freezing weather so there would be no burst pipes, report any leaks in the roof, keep the rooms cleaned enough to avoid heavy accumulations of dust, make a list of furniture or other items that needed replacing or repairing. None of it sounded beyond my ability, which was a relief.

"I wonder if I might get into town before the weather gets bad," I said. "I've thought of several things I'd like to have."

"Someone will be going in this week," my hostess promised. "Get whatever you like in the way of food and bill it to the ranch. Also, during the winter you can have orders filled by one of our men. We're never snowed in really tight for more than several weeks. Even then we can get around on snowmobiles, so it's not as ferocious as you might expect.

"It's just dull as hell," came a voice from behind me.

Cecile strode over, now wearing brushed corduroy flared jeans, snugged low on the hips with a broad belt. She wore a pucker-knit emerald green shirt and broad-strapped sandals. Plopping into the damask silver chair beside her mother, the girl took two rolls and almost forced them into her mouth.

"Cecile!" began Mrs. Lindsay. "You really—" She bit off her words, giving me a helpless look. "Someone once said, Jan, that young people should be locked off from the rest of the world between the ages of ten and twenty-three, and I swear that I agree." To her daughter she said pleadingly, "You don't have to stay here winters, love. You'd be much better off at a girls' school where you'd have friends your own age, fun, activities—"

"I'll never have friends my own age," Cecile observed. "The girls are silly and the boys are babies! I just wish I were grown up and could do what I wanted."

Her mother's eyes narrowed. "If you think I do what I want ..." she flamed, then drew on her third cigarette, managing a wry laugh. "You'll grow up soon enough. Meanwhile, if you won't board in town or go to a girls' school, you must do your lessons. Day by day, no getting behind the way you did last year. Have you done anything today?"

"I slept till ten," yawned Cecile, munching another roll. "And I'm going with Colin and Tam this afternoon to check on the cattle in the high pasture."

"Not till you do your lessons."

"Colin said I could go!"

"Colin has no jurisdiction over your schooling and home life," Shana Lindsay said curtly, looking rather flushed. "Unfortunately, I have to see to that."

"But—"

Mrs. Lindsay glanced at her sinuous gold bracelet watch. "If you worked hard, you could catch up with the men later this afternoon and ride back with them."

Tears of frustrated rage glinted in Cecile's green eyes.

She flung herself up, rattling the china on the tray, and ran for the door.

"You—you hateful old woman!" she cried, halting in the door to hurl a challenge. "You—you're jealous of me. You just don't want me to be with Colin!"

Shana Lindsay got to her feet, suddenly looking almost haggard. "Another remark like that, Cecile, and you *will* go to boarding school, perhaps in England!"

"But I don't understand that silly geometry," wailed the girl, cowed into childishness again.

"I'm not a teacher," her mother said. "Perhaps your father—"

"Britt's your husband!" spat Cecile. "He's not my father! Maybe Colin will help me with all those obtuse angles and hypotenuses."

"Cecile," Shana decreed, "occasional help from Colin would be fine, if he were willing. But you'd use this as a way to smother him in that ridiculous way, embarrass him, cause problems. I forbid you to ask him."

"Then who's going to explain it?" Cecile demanded sullenly.

"Britt could."

"No! I hate him! I—"

"Do the work yourself, then, or get packed to stay in town for the school term." Mrs. Lindsay turned her back on her daughter and rang the bell.

I found myself saying quietly, "Mrs. Lindsay, would you mind if I helped Cecile? I'm not great at geometry, but I think I remember enough to worry it out with her."

Mrs. Lindsay eyed me in real shock. "You—you're volunteering?" she asked incredulously. "After you've seen how obnoxious she is?"

"She *is* hard to take," I agreed. "And I wouldn't put up with tantrums. But I'll have plenty of time, and after all, my profession will be that of teaching. It might be fun to get some practice."

"Well, Cecile?" asked the mistress of Smoke Valley. "I hope you appreciate this. It's very kind of Miss Richardson, especially when she's seen you at your worst."

The girl ignored her mother, fixing those enormous cat's eyes on me. "Could—could you help me a little while now?"

I looked inquiringly at Mrs. Lindsay, who shrugged. "Don't feel you must plunge in today, Jan."

Cecile's eyes pleaded. I moved toward her. "Let's have a look at your textbook," I said, laughing, "and see how much they've changed methods since I was your age."

An hour of concentrated study pulled Cecile through that day's assignment. She actually understood more than she thought she did, but lacked the patience to apply and follow through. Her manner, as we worked at the desk in her upstairs room, was positively angelic, though she sent me a number of warily oblique glances.

Thrusting the geometry to  one side, she said, "Thanks, Miss Richardson. I can get this history outline done real fast and still go with Tam and Colin."

"Great," I said, rising. "When you get stuck, come over. Maybe you'd better call first just in case I go out for a walk."

"Sure." Cecile grinned broadly, for the first time looking her age, revealing the basic child beneath her nymphet swagger. "If you enjoy walks, I'll take you to some places you wouldn't find otherwise."

"I'd like that, Cecile. Good-bye for now."

" 'Bye," she murmured; already intent on her notebook and a fat textbook.

I closed the door on her room, which was done in purple, mauve and aqua, postered on every available inch. It was filled with the not-quite-discarded games and fashion dolls of preadolescence, jammed up alongside teen-age paraphernalia; records, tape recorder, loop radio in screaming pink, stacks of magazines and paperbacks. On the door was a sign lettered in blatant orange: *XXX Rated—No Grups Allowed.*

There was, I decided, more child than siren in the girl, though the balance was getting closer. And I was glad Tam Cannon would be with her and Colin that afternoon. Tam wouldn't be above rebuking or even spanking her if she got aggressively seductive, but I doubted that with him close she'd even try.

"Miss Richardson?" came a voice from the bottom of the stairs.

Startled, I looked down into Britt Lindsay's light russet eyes. He smiled charmingly. "Please," he said, in that gentle, attractive voice with its faint difference in accent. "Won't you join us for lunch?"

# 6

The dining room had shuttered windows opening the length of the wall on a view of the mountains. The other walls were paneled in cedar, which gave out a fragrant aroma, and the floor was inlaid in different colors of wood, with a border of some almost white wood about a foot from the walls.

Tapestries hung on every wall, faded with age, beautiful in mellowed colors of rose, blue, green, and yellow on the aged backing. The tapestries at the ends of the room were biblical—David and Goliath, Cain and Abel—but the large one that held pride of place and must have been fifteen feet long was of unicorns, one drinking at a fountain, one lying on its forelegs, a third trustfully lowering his graceful head with its golden horn into a maiden's lap. Behind her, the lady held a knife, but the unicorn did not see that.

I was glad that Britt Lindsay had seated me facing the windows. The table was huge, and though we sat at one end of it, Britt at the head, his wife and I facing each other, we were still too far apart for comfortable passing of dishes.

Gleaming silver, gold-banded china, sparkling crystal, snowy napkins folded into silver holders shaped like true-lovers' knots—the whole dining room seemed out of place in this wild jagged country. At a long sideboard, Britt asked if I preferred white or red wine.

"Whatever you're having," I murmured, rather overwhelmed by such state for everyday.

"Mrs. Lindsay drinks only sauterne, which I wouldn't advise unless you're fond of it," Britt said. "Try my Beaujolais."

He filled my glass with the rich dark wine, then poured a white wine into his wife's. When he had filled his own glass and was seated, she raised her glass and smiled.

"For me, there is no other wine, Jan."

"Yes," agreed Britt, with an edge of malice. "For your Chateau D'Yquem, grapes have to be picked so overripe they're almost, but not quite, rotten. *Au moment critique*, isn't it? Your French is better than mine."

"You have it precisely, dear," she answered, sipping appreciatively as Paula trundled in a cart loaded with food. "But then, your moments are always critical, aren't they? Because you are."

Britt ignored that gibe. "Paula," he said, "where is Cecile?"

"She got some bread and cheese, Mr. Britt, and ran off to catch Tam and Colin."

So it was, for the two cousins of Lindsay blood, *Mr.* Britt and Colin. Paula moved out, graceful as a willow walking, and Britt passed me a tray of various meats, turkey, ham and beef, as he remarked to his wife in a brittle tone, "That girl is likely to catch more than a canter after the cattle if she keeps chasing Colin, my dear."

Again that flush came over Shana Lindsay's creamy skin. "Nonsense, Britt! Colin's her uncle."

"Not by blood, love, not by blood."

Was there an emphasis on the way he said *blood?* Now his wife was pale, her face drained of color except for her lipstick and rouge, which had before been perfectly blended to her flesh. She took a long sip of her wine.

"Colin has looked after Cecile ever since she was eight years old," she insisted. "He's not the man to act out perversities."

This time I thought there was an underlining of *perversities*. Britt shrugged and passed the crystal leaf tray of celery stuffed with pimiento cheese, carrot curls, radish rosettes, ripe and green olives, and sliced tomatoes. Mrs. Lindsay sliced from a loaf of crusty brown bread and offered me some from the plate. I took a piece and a small cut of each of the four kinds of cheese on a ceramic board. I was no cheese connoisseur, but the bits tasted perfect of their kind: the Muenster bland, cheddar sharp, port wine creamy, and the white feta just the right shade acrid. The meats were sliced thin but retained flavor and juiciness, and there was no raw vegetable I didn't like.

But in spite of the appetizing food and its tempting way of being served, I didn't feel hungry. Even though their voices stayed civil and pleasant, there was an atmosphere between the Lindsays that made me acutely uncomfortable.

"That Jamaican blood of your daughter's is likely to come out," said Britt, coolly returning to the siege. "They mature early, don't they? After all, dear, you only lived there the first seven years of your life, but after that even ten years of chill Church of England prim-and-proper boarding schools couldn't starch it out of you, could it?"

"England!" she cried. "That's where—" And for a shattering moment, her adult face was that of the frightened girl in the hall portrait, staring as if sightless at the fox's tail.

"You were of English parentage on both sides," Britt went on relentlessly. "But you're a mutant, of course. And Cecile's father—he *was* Jamaican, wasn't he? Or are you sure?"

I pushed back my chair, rising. "Excuse me," I said. "I'd better be going."

I was almost at the door when Shana Lindsay's voice reached after me. "Please, Jan, come back and have your lunch. Really, Britt, it's terribly rude of you to behave like this in front of a guest!"

"It is." Britt was in front of me swiftly with that melting, boyish smile, a light, coaxing hand on my elbow. "Do sit down, my dear. We rustics forget our manners once the summer people leave. We work off all the hostile feelings accumulated since the last chance we had time and place to snarl. But we shouldn't distress you with it. Stay a while, and we'll be ever so entertaining."

There seemed no graceful way out. Besides, there had been a definite note of pleading in Mrs. Lindsay's request, which was strange, because of the two I would have cast her as the aggressor, the one who sharpened tongue and ego on the other.

The rest of the meal passed in small talk and not particularly probing questions about me. Certainly if either of them felt any unease about both Anne and me coming from the same state, it didn't show. By the end of the meal, they had asked me to call them Shana and Britt.

"We're not *that* much older," she said graciously, "and though we have to maintain a certain distance with lodge personnel in the summer, simply because there are about twenty of them, we like to be friends with our winter keeper—out of self-interest! Otherwise she might get lonely and depart."

"And you wouldn't care to be the winter keeper, would you, darling?" teased Britt.

She lifted her slim shoulders and smiled. "I must confess to being a total coward about staying alone," she confided. "I think you're very brave. But you young American women have been brought up so much differently than I—"

Britt's laughter interrupted. "No one else was ever brought up like you, Shana!"

She gave him a little smile, then said to Paula, who

was clearing away, "We'll have coffee on the sun porch, please." And to me, "There won't be many more days warm enough for that. It's nice that you got here in time to see the autumn colors and get an idea of how it looks without that cold white snow blanket."

"Ah, but winter's the real time here," Britt said, following us as Shana led the way through the hall and a side passage that opened on a long screened porch at the back of the house. "And that blanket's not always white. People still remember the green snow of 1933, and there's been red snow, too. Algae caused both."

I frowned, then realized that he wasn't making this up for my benefit. I looked around the porch. The stone floors were splashed with Indian blankets and straw matting, and the furniture was rawhide and peeled cedar.

"What tables!" I exclaimed in wonder.

Besides a number of small rawhide drum tables scattered around the porch to hold drinks and ashtrays, there were two unique tables. One was at least eight feet long, shaped like an irregular island, with bark still around the edges. It was set on small log legs, and the surface was polished till the circles radiating from the cortex shone with glimmering variations: time, its wet and dry seasons, incarnate in wood.

The other masterpiece was a three-inch-thick slab of what looked like patterned marble set on a wrought-iron frame. It was three feet in diameter, white, veined with carnelian, purple, and ochre.

"Petrified wood," Britt explained. "Not many slabs that fine left outside of restricted park areas. The slicing and polishing often wreck a slab, too, so that one like this retails for about two thousand dollars, when one can be had. The other table is of redwood. Tam made it. Woodwork's his hobby."

"He's—he's really an artist," I breathed, caressing the lacquered bark of the table's edge.

"Don't let him hear you say that," Shana warned laughingly. "Tam can't see and he can't hear, but his people have been here since white men came, and he's first, last, and eternally a cowboy."

"Eternal is right," Britt said. "I think every winter's going to be his last, but come spring here he is again.

"Tam has a winter cabin up on the north range," Shana explained. "He forts up about the end of October and keeps an eye on things there until the snows melt. Uses snowshoes, old as he is. He hates snowmobiles."

"Yes, but he's glad enough to get the fresh stuff we get in to him by snowmobile," said Britt.

We lingered over coffee until what had been pleasant relaxation grew heavy, protracted; perhaps my employers didn't want to make the first move at ending the visit.

"This has been delightful," I said, rising from a laced rawhide chair. "Thank you very much."

Britt looked up at me. "Are you interested in hibernation?" he asked abruptly.

"Hibernation?" I echoed, totally surprised. "I'm afraid I really don't know much about it."

"It's one of the great mysteries," Britt said. "At least as puzzling as migration for creatures who can't stand the cold. Why do some hibernate and some migrate? And for that matter, how is it possible for a creature to live in a state of almost suspended animation for five or six months? Why does size vary from that of bear to squirrel? Why don't pikas hibernate? Why—"

"Oh, good God!" exclaimed Shana. "This is where I go out. See you later, Jan, drop over any time you like. It's most kind of you to coach that daughter of mine in geometry." She offered a slender hand in a friendly, light clasp. "If Britt's hibernation craze drives you up the wall, just plead a headache—which you might have by then—and do what I think Cecile calls 'split'!"

She vanished in a smooth, flowing walk. Her husband's eyes followed her, and I wondered again what their relationship was. Tinctured with hostility, for certain, barbed with knowledge of each other, troubled by

Cecile's existence. But what else lay between them, what was the taste and fashion and balance of their love? If it was love ...

"Are you bored?" asked Britt.

"No," I said truthfully. "I like animals. But I'm a city girl, I really don't know much about them." I smiled. "Those pikas are absolute darlings, though. I'd love to see them up close."

"You're in the right place." Britt laughed, his enthusiasm mounting again. Why did women, even nice ones, need to cut their men down as Shana had? Jealousy? Disguised attack motivated by buried or inadmissible reasons? "Come along. We have a colony of them near my lab."

"Lab?"

"Yes." He had opened the porch door, and as we walked along a flagstone path threading between birdbaths, raked-over flower beds, and stands of still-blooming shrubs, he said in a wistful tone that might have come from a boy, "Ranching and the lodge were just what I had to do, Jan, because they were in the family. But at school I studied zoology and science, and in my free time, I keep my hand in."

"Couldn't your cousin manage the ranch?" I asked.

"Colin?" Britt gave a dismissing shrug. "Colin—well, he has a few habits that don't mix well with steady responsibility, though he's one of the best cattle-breeders in the country. Anyway, it's not my fault that his mother, my esteemed aunt, never bothered to formalize her union with a gay young Air Force pilot before he got killed in stunt-diving. She took his name unofficially, but the Lindsays are strong on clean bloodlines. Colin inherited cash, but he won't get the ranch unless I have no heir." Between his teeth, he added, "That seems to appear more likely year by year."

Lack of a child, then, could explain a lot of the ambiguous warfare between him and his wife. We passed through an iron gate, taking a path that led into the high, thick pines, and after perhaps ten minutes came upon a massive slide of rocks that had spilled sometime from the giant cliff above. A few small trees and shrubs had survived in the shifting rubble, but sunlight fell directly on most of the ledges and miniature precipices.

"There's a pile of hay!" I cried in delight, pointing at a heap several feet high.

"And here comes some more." Britt grinned.

A bright-eyed plump little animal was coming along a ledge, head high, its mouth open to unbelievable width to hold a large bunch of brilliant autumn flowers.

"Just like a bouquet," I whispered.

It ran into a rock jumble. In a moment, another pika emerged from the other direction. He dragged a long stem, well over a yard long, and deposited it in the first pile.

"They'll be moving their hay inside very quickly now," said Britt.

"What do they collect?"

"Depends on the region, it seems. That pile is probably about half grass and half huckleberry stems and leaves. In Idaho, sagebrush is the staple; around Jackson Hole, it's elder leaves; and there was a pile found in New Mexico that contained thirty-four different plants. Seems to vary among colonies, too, just as food habits do with humans. Some colonies specialize in a few plants, while others gather almost everything edible."

"Doesn't the hay mildew?"

"No, they add the plants little by little so that a pile cures as it grows." Britt laughed. "Some scientists from one of the universities have studied the pikas' hay-making for tips on improved methods of curing fodder. So you see, mankind hasn't got all the skills!"

"You know a lot about them," I said, warming to him more than I had before we sighted the pikas.

"That's because they're interesting," Britt said. "Now, will you step into my parlor?" He waved toward a cabin I hadn't noticed, partly because of my absorption in the pikas, partly because it was shielded by a ledge and close-growing pines.

We walked around to the door on the other side and stepped into a large, long room that would have made very comfortable living quarters. The rug was thick, a warm rose color, while the upholstered chairs and sofa grouped around the stone fireplace were done in snuff and violet—not exactly what one would expect to find in a mountain cabin, but most attractive nonetheless. The curtains were snuff, and a counter in the same color cut off a compact but complete kitchen from the work area that filled the main part of the room—several desks, a big table littered with stacks of papers, a filing cabinet, several full wastebaskets, a shelf of books.

"The laboratory is through there." Britt nodded in the direction of the kitchen. "Would you like a look first, or could I make you a drink?" He slid open a cabinet stocked with more bottles than I had ever before seen outside a bar or liquor store.

"Thanks, the wine was enough for me," I said. "I don't drink much."

"Time for you to need to later," Britt said, pouring out straight whiskey and downing it in a gulp. "All right! To the lab!"

He opened the door and stood back to let me enter a room as large as the first. It was windowed from waist height to ceiling all the way around, except for the wall adjoining the kitchen, but long fluorescent lights ran across the room as well.

There were microscopes and various surgical-looking tools on the several long plastic-topped counters. Everything was antiseptically white and clean, including the lineoleum floor. But a row of cages ran along the wall on one side of the room. My heart went icy cold. I hate cages, even for canaries.

Bending, I peered through the screen and saw a little rodent in the first container. A squirrel was next to him, then a chipmunk, then several waking rabbits, more squirrels, more animals like the first, and a few bats.

"What are you doing with them?" I demanded, unable to keep a condemnatory note from my voice even if I'd tried. "Why are there so many?"

I turned to find him watching me with a strange light in those pale amber eyes.

# 7

"I'm trying to find out what causes hibernation," he said, after a pause that lengthened till the chill in my heart spread through my body and I felt really afraid of him, though certainly there was no menace in his posture or manner. "Biologists and scientists have been working on the secret for decades, but they haven't yet found an answer that holds up."

"What difference does that make?" I asked. "What possible good—"

"It would make a lot of difference, if we knew how to induce true hibernation," Britt interrupted. "For example, in an area threatened with famine, injections could keep people alive until the next harvest—they wouldn't need food for months! And in certain crisis situations, hibernation might avert death, say, when oxygen was limited in a spaceship or submarine or underground area—trapped miners, maybe. Hibernating creatures use minute amounts of oxygen. They can be left in water for as long as an hour or sealed in airtight jars for the same time without apparent damage. Also, induced hibernation might be of great help in treating certain mental disorders. It seems that the brain ceases to function too—there's deep dreamless sleep. A month or two of that might solve a lot of people's problems, enable them to heal from emotional or physical wounds. And it could be useful in treating certain diseases. There's no end to the possibilities once the mystery is revealed."

Forced to acknowledge the potential, I still didn't like the cages. My expression must have said as much, for Britt laughed and rested his hand on the cage of the rodent who seemed fast asleep, though some of the squirrels were chattering and the rabbits nibbled at the lettuce in their cages.

"My dear, I haven't killed a research animal yet. I just subject the hibernators to various tests during the sleep season and keep careful notes on them, as opposed to the rabbits, who are my control specimens."

"How long have you been doing this?" I asked.

"On a serious scale, for about three years. And I have verified some very interesting facts. Hibernating animals have an unusual distribution of calcium and magnesium in their blood. Chilled injections of insulin and magnesium will induce pseudo-hibernation in animals that don't hibernate, but the animal will die in its slumber if not treated with counteractive drugs."

"I thought you said you hadn't killed anything."

He shrugged. "Only a cat died. Then I injected the others and they were no worse for wear. Hell, sweet child, how many cats are gassed or killed every day at your Humane Society? Isn't it better there's some purpose to their death?"

"I still don't like it."

Again those eyes grew strange. "Then I'm most disappointed in you," he said curtly, turning on his heel, though he punctiliously let me precede him into the living area. "I thought you were an intelligent woman with some notion of realities."

I didn't have any answer to that, only feelings, and his words stung. The warming I had felt toward him at his understanding of the pikas had faded completely.

"Will you have the drink now?" he asked, voice taunting.

"No, thank you. I really must get back to the lodge."

"Come along, then. I'll drive you from the ranch."

"That's kind, but I'd enjoy the walk now that I know the way."

"Please yourself."

My hand was on the door when he spoke again in a wistful, almost sad way that touched me in spite of my dislike of his laboratory.

"Nature is such a deep wonderful mystery, and hibernation—that state between life and death, on the thin edge—is so fascinating, so potentially gift-giving to man, that I hoped you'd understand. I don't hurt the animals, you know."

"It is a miracle," I said. "And perhaps you're right, perhaps the secret could help people in extreme situations. But I still don't like—" and I broke off, gesturing toward the lab.

He bowed his silver-blond head in assent, but said in quick pleading, "If I could just talk to you about it—the way we talked of the pikas. It does bring sparks and new ideas out, to put thoughts in words, to have to explain them." He smiled very winningly. "If I tried to tell you what I know, I'd discover that I know a lot more than I now do, consciously. It'd sweep off the cobwebs, shine up my thoughts."

I hesitated a minute. What he had just told me about hibernation did intrigue me. And he wasn't a vivisectionist, or imprisoning animals for the fun of it. Besides, I ate meat, liked it, and had no intention of stopping. Why should I pull holier-than-thou with Britt?

Too, the more I could see of the family, become close to them, the more likely I was to learn about Anne, or at least Nordstrom.

"I'd be interested in learning all I can," I said, speaking on two levels. And then, sounding like a put-down though I didn't mean it that way, "Thank you for showing me the pikas."

His mouth quirked. There was a fragile look about him, as if he might break if knocked against roughly. "You're welcome," he said, and as I left, I could sense that he was standing in the door, watching after me with those strange russet eyes.

I walked briskly, drawing the clean, tingling air into my lungs, seeing the golden aspens, dark pines, spills of rock, goldenrod, and late flowers as clearly as if my eyes had been washed with a fluid that let them see with transfiguring clarity. I passed the gated entrance to the ranch house, for Britt's cabin was reached by the continuing road that ran from the lodge to the ranch, and kept going on the way that took me past Colin's place.

A pair of young black dogs ran out, barking happily, wagging their tails. They were half-grown, I decided, from the proportion of their paws to the rest of them. They had thick, smooth hair, and I thought they were some kind of Labrador. I patted and spoke to them and they stopped barking, escorting me for a while, sometimes gamboling ahead, often racing and cavorting, but when we reached the fork of the road to Billings, they turned as if on signal and loped back the way we had come.

Colin's dogs?

Sorry that they had left me, for I like dogs in an almost totally indiscriminate way, I took the branch toward the lodge. It was late afternoon when I stopped for a moment to admire the pinnacled mineral terrace, then went up the steps. I was leg-weary, and my head was jumbled, too, full of impressions of that fantastic English manor house in the middle of the wilderness, and even more confusing, the people I had met.

Going back to the kitchen, I took off my shoes, rubbed my toes, and made some hot chocolate which I carried into the big main hall, determined to overcome some of my spookiness about it.

I took an easy chair close to a window, put my feet up on a table, and sipped the hot relaxing drink while the people I had met that day drifted through my mind.

Shana Lindsay, so elegant and assured, yet with that edge of panic that showed on the face of the girl in the hall painting. Calm, quiet Paula. Tam Cannon with his shrewd, kindly expression. Cecile, child of a Jamaican, hating her stepfather, obviously centering her starved love on Colin. A Botticelli angel with a bright Afro and mermaid eyes, and a budding, lithe, delicious body.

I sighed so heavily that it surprised me. Why should I feel such sympathy with a girl who had been almost insulting, who was clearly a terror to deal with? True, she had responded a little when I had helped her with her geometry, but I knew her problems were too great, too involved and deeply rooted in the lives of the adults, for me to change her outlook.

Would she come tomorrow to study? I sighed again. Even for me, it was easier to explain the measurement and relationships of points, angles, surfaces, and solids than to teach a girl like that one about the relationships of people. I doubted if Colin had had better luck. Old Tam could probably do more in that line than anyone else around here. I hoped I'd see him again before he went up to his winter quarters at the north end of the ranch.

Britt's face rose before my eyes. What was he really? A throwback to bloodlines too delicate for this country? Potential discoverer of a secret that could save whole populations from starving, or simply an ineffective man using his "experiments" as an ego prop while his at least partially disinherited cousin supervised the ranch?

Of course, if Britt had no children, then Colin would inherit. In fact, if Britt died now, the ranch would probably go to his cousin after suitable provision was made for Shana.

Did Colin think about that?

It was getting dusky. I could no longer make out the many-hued but predominantly white sculptured terraced formation across the front clearing. Rising, I made sure the door was locked, put the key back under the mask, and looked in the direction of Colin's home.

Either he wasn't there or it wasn't dark enough yet to make out a light. I drifted back to the kitchen, switched on the light, and decided to have scrambled eggs for dinner.

The wind had come up, and the lodge creaked and groaned. I carried my plate to my bedroom, turned on the television, and for a while I could almost pretend I was back home. When the program ended, I turned on the kitchen radio to mask eerie noises while I did dishes, and then, transistor playing, I wrote Mother a long letter.

It had to be long. There was much to tell, and besides, as Britt Lindsay had said, in telling and thinking about what you know, you may discover facets or angles overlooked before.

But my letter brought no helpful discoveries, no answers to the complexities of the people here, or fresh insights on Anne. By the time I was ready for bed, I was so sleepy that I dropped off in spite of all the disturbing sounds, the shrill whining of the wind.

Had it helped to pull the drapes and look out to be assured that through the woods a light shone in Colin's house?

Next morning I put Mother's letter in the mailbox outside the lodge. I was writing her in care of a friend who lived out of town who was serving as a forwarder of mail for us both so that no one at Smoke Valley could notice that Anne and I got letters from the same person.

Then I surveyed the building and made a schedule of maintenance cleaning, for even though my job was a cover, I intended to do it well. In addition to the cleaning things downstairs, there was a closet at either end of the upstairs wings which contained a vacuum cleaner, dust cloths, polish, and other supplies.

Mrs. Lindsay had said that the rooms only needed cleaning every six weeks or so, enough to keep dust from building up. I apportioned the work so that if I did about six rooms a week, and then spent several days out of a month on the downstairs area, I could very handily keep up with what was needed, with plenty of free time.

It was almost noon by the time I had done my computing, but I decided to start on the left upstairs wing and do at least one room before lunch.

It took only a half-hour to vacuum the small room and whisk a polish cloth over the furniture. Dutifully picking up the room plan, I checked the bathroom but saw nothing that needed repair or replacement so long as one didn't worry about glass rings and minor cigarette burns on the furniture—and Shana Lindsay had told me not to.

I was vacuuming under the bed in the next room when there was a click and a chewing sound. Turning off the machine, I pulled out the head and tried to locate whatever had been sucked into it. Something fell out, nicked and bent but still in one piece, so I hoped that the innards of the vacuum were too.

I glanced casually at the bludgeoned metal ring in my hand. I looked again, raising it slowly, turning it so that the enameled crest showed. A class ring from Anne's high school, with her graduation year blazoned on it.

It was just not very likely that anyone else from that school and year had been at Smoke Valley.

I stared at it, trembling, wishing there were some way to make it speak. Of course there was probably not much to tell. Anne must have lost it when cleaning the room.

But it had been in such an inaccessible place, back against the wall beneath the shell of the bookcase headboard. I couldn't stop the picture that flashed through my mind. Anne lying on this bed with a man—

No! She had just lost the ring while cleaning.

But I opened all the drawers, searched closet shelves and bathroom medicine cabinet, hunting vainly for some trace of whoever had been in this room.

Nothing.

I tucked the ring in the pocket of my jeans, collected the cleaning things, and then put them in the next room, ready to use when I next came upstairs. Then I moved slowly down the hall to the balcony, dim even at this brightest part of the day, and went downstairs.

There must be a registry, some record of who had

stayed when in what room. But was it here or at the ranch, or locked up someplace for safety till next season?

The registration and information counter in one corner of the main hall had a subdivided open mailbox behind it. Several drawers under the counter failed to yield more than pencils, pens, stamps, paper clips, memo pads, and such. But in a larger drawer at the bottom of the counter, I found four big books. Sitting on the floor, I opened one.

It was a register, but several years old. The third book proved to be last summer's. I checked through it, mouth dry, heart pounding.

About halfway through the book, entered for Room 202, the one where I had found the ring, was the signature of Lars Nordstrom.

My eyes blurred, my heart beating with a slow fatal dread as I blinked to clear my vision and read the checkout time. August 9, two days before we'd had Nordstrom's telegram.

Time for him to have taken Anne to California.

The address was the same fictitious one in Minnesota. I checked the other registers; every summer Nordstrom had come to stay for a month or more.

I put the books back. Well, if he were that frequent a guest, just as Shana Lindsay had claimed, any steady help, such as the lodge cook, would know him. The trouble was, no regular lodge help was here. Hope dimmed.

Possibly, just possibly, Tam Cannon might know him. And Colin McReynolds well might. But Colin was one of the family. If anything was off-key, he might not tell what he knew. I didn't think Old Tam could or would lie, though.

I'd ask him.

Still kneeling, I suddenly wondered if other records were kept here—names of employees, wages, reasons for dismissal, and so on. The shelves that stretched from the mail partitioning to the floor were divided into open files jammed with papers, brochures, manila envelopes, ledgers—it would be a long job going through that mess, but if a record were kept in the lodge, it would most likely be right there.

When I'd been cleaning that last room, I'd been very hungry, but now my appetite was gone. I reached for the newest-looking ledger.

"What are you doing?" demanded a voice from behind.

# 8

Jerking my hand back from the ledger as if the book had sprouted fangs, I jumped up to look into Cecile's curious green eyes.

"Oh," I gulped, trying wildly to think of something plausible, "I—I was just cleaning and thought these shelves could use a tidying."

"They always can," chuckled Cecile, deciding to smile so that two dimples starred her cheeks and made her even more bewitching. "Did you mean what you said? About helping with my—*yeech!* geometry?"

"Of course." I came around the counter. "Mind if I have a sandwich while we work?"

"If you'll give me one, too," said Cecile. "I left the table while I was still in the middle of my shrimp cocktail. That horrid, sleazy, weaselly man! Why did Mother have to go and marry him?"

I bypassed this outburst because I simply didn't know a helpful thing to say, let alone a discreet one.

"What do you like?" I asked, producing spreads, cheese, and meats from the refrigerator, and slicing the home-baked loaf. "Make your own delight."

Cecile heaped on ham, beef, mayonnaise, olives, cheese, and pickles, but she did not forget her grudge.

Hooking one skinny but shapely leg over around a stool, she sat there and took a precarious bite, chewed, and swallowed, and spoke the instant her mouth was empty.

"He's got no right to treat me the way he does, damn him! I don't want to eat like a 'civilized' person in that silly old European way. I'm an American! I'll never leave this country except to go to Jamaica, maybe, so what do I care about his stupid old table etiquette?"

She was certainly not worrying about anything now except devouring her food, so I skirted the aggrieved query and asked, "Would you like some hot chocolate? I'm addicted to it."

"Sure, long as I don't have to stir it."

Fortified with chocolate and a sandwich that rivaled Cecile's apart from the pickles and olives, I looked at the text she had opened, and we began our study.

An hour and a half later, Cecile doubled her work papers, stuck them in the book, and shook herself all over like a kitten coming out of an unwelcome dunking.

"Would you like to go walking?" she asked. "There's time to go to some of the fumaroles and geysers."

"What are fumaroles?"

"They're—well, they're holes that vapor and gas come out of," she explained.

Cecile seldom tried to define things, see them distinctly as parts. But when, as in geometry, she focused her acute if vagabond intelligence, she could perform mental feats she normally would refuse to attempt as being beyond her.

A wild child allowed to grow wilder, with the charm, originality, and boorishness of such. But she wouldn't be a child long. She needed to learn some controls to keep from wrecking herself. Her mother and stepfather obviously roused rebellion on principle, and Colin's influence was distorted by her passion for him, fueled in great part, I suspected, by her fiercely rejected need for a father. Apart from myself, possibly, only Old Tam seemed to have any chance of giving the girl some disinterested affection and balance.

I certainly didn't feel equal to Cecile's need, but who else was there? Besides, I could do with some company myself in what threatened to be a long, isolated winter pursuing the haunting mystery of my young sister.

"Let's go," I said.

To my surprise, Cecile caught my hand, pulled me along, and by the time we reached the clearing out front, we were running and laughing as I had not since Anne and I were children together.

"What makes the colors?" I asked, pulling up short at the terrace opposite the lodge, admiring again the subtle shadings of the layers.

Cecile cast me an impatient glance, then sighed and collected what she knew. "It's algae," she said. "The temperature of the water determines the color." She thought some more. "Colin wrote it all down for me once. Let's see: the white happens at a hundred eighty-five degrees, flesh-pink is a few degrees less, then the pale yellow is about one sixty-five with yellow-green about ten degrees less. There isn't any emerald here, or orange or red or brown, but you'll see these in other places where the temperatures are lower."

"Marvelous," I said, letting her draw me away and out of the clearing. "But you're used to it, I suppose."

"Yes, I'm used to breathing, too, but I still need it. I'll bet you don't have anything like this where you came from."

"You're right. Though it's beautiful country in its timbered, rivered way."

"You're from Missouri, aren't you?"

"Yes."

Cecile's face spasmed. "There was a girl from there worked at the lodge last summer," she said. "Of course, she was from St. Louis. I don't suppose you knew her."

My heart was going like a trip-hammer. "Still, there's a chance. What was her name?"

"Anne. Anne Dupree."

I turned my face as if to watch distant peaks. Careful

now, careful. Cecile's expression had given away some strong emotion for Anne and it didn't seem pleasant.

"Unusual name," I remarked in a flat tone, going to some trouble not to lie. "I'm sure I couldn't have forgotten it if I'd known her."

"She was pretty," Cecile almost accused.

"So are lots of girls."

"Not the way she was."

"Did you see much of her?"

Cecile arched golden eyebrows. "Me? How could I? She spent all her free time with—with Colin." His name was wrenched from her as if torn from her heart.

My own heart thudded till I was dizzy, slightly sick. Anne with Colin? Then where did Nordstrom come in? I burned to ask but couldn't do so directly. "I should think she would have made friends with guests at the lodge," I ventured.

Cecile gave me a look of scorn. "When she could be with Colin?"

I tried another tack. "Does your mother discourage friendships between guests and lodge workers?"

"Not unless the guest is someone she wants," said the girl in an indifferent way. "Of course she always tells the staff that favoritism is not allowed and that frolics can't go on during duty hours."

"But this Anne left at the end of the season?"

"Earlier." Cecile's scowl vanished and she laughed in triumph. "I woke up one morning and she was gone. Mother says she went off with some guest. Colin didn't believe it for a while, but I guess something convinced him. He's still terribly grim, but he'll get over her soon and—and I'm getting older all the time."

Now my mind really whirred, sorting the pieces, trying them here and there. Anne had left before the end of the season; she and Colin had spent a lot of time together; Cecile had been wildly jealous. But then where did Nordstrom fit in, the man whose sojourns at the lodge were vouched for by the registers? If Anne had liked Colin all that well, I couldn't imagine her getting involved with another man at the same time, much less going off with him for a vacation.

As Cecile went in front of me across a narrow unrailed foot log above a swift dark stream, I had to think how easy it would be for one of us to have an accident out here, a fatal one. If I shoved Cecile right now, for instance . . .

What with boiling hot vapor holes, precipices, and rock slides, it wouldn't be hard to dispose of a body. Only Anne's body had been found in California.

If she had been killed here, why had she been taken there? Obviously to deflect suspicion. Shana Lindsay would have to have known of any such trick, but she would probably lie to protect her daughter.

My mind whirred again, stopping with a terrified click. Colin might have done it if Anne had dropped him for Nordstrom, done it in some goaded moment of jealousy and rage. Shana would cover up for him, and Cecile, for certain, would never tell on her idol.

My scalp crawled. There seemed to be no end of suspects. Shana, if she had had an affair going with Colin, might have killed my sister, assisted by this mysterious Nordstrom.

Or it could possibly be all as Shana had told Mother and me. I *had* found Anne's ring in that inaccessible space beneath the bed in Nordstrom's room.

I couldn't see any particular motivation for Britt to be mixed up in anything that might have happened. He could perfectly well not even have known, absorbed as he was in his experiments. I didn't think it likely that he'd want to protect either Colin or Cecile. Or his wife, either, the wife who had produced no heirs.

The only person I felt I could trust around Smoke Valley was Tam Cannon, but he almost surely knew nothing. I couldn't imagine his hushing a girl's murder to save anyone. Paula served in the house and knew what she knew. It would be a long time, if ever, before she would talk about her knowledge.

Gaining the other side of the foot log, on which I had kept a careful distance from my guide, since pushing *could* come abruptly from the front as well as from behind, I decided that a number of things—including the one advanced by Shana—might have happened to Anne. And there were, on present evidence, four possible killers: Cecile, Shana, Colin and Nordstrom.

Since I, cut off from everything and everyone familiar, would be snowed in near these people all winter, I had better be extremely careful with them until and if the Nordstrom story proved to be true.

But I hated living with suspicion. Here I was, even suspecting that the girl dropping back beside me now, face frank and eager, might possibly have done away with my sister Anne. Cecile pointed west to where I caught a moving glint, making out birds who must have been very large to be seen from such a distance.

"Swans!" Cecile cried. "And I'll bet they're some of the trumpeters. Maybe we can get over to their lake before travel gets bad. Or I could take you in the snowmobile."

"Don't swans migrate?"I asked.

"Not these. The underground heat that causes the steam and fumaroles and geysers keeps the water at a livable temperature for them. They are positively absolutely swinging far-out birds!"

*Could* she have killed Anne?

In spite of the terrible doubt, I warmed to her enthusiasm, to the fiery spirit powering that skinny someday-woman-yet-now-most-vulnerable-body.

"Do you have any—" I almost said playmates, but checked myself. "Any friends up here?"

"Tam and Paula. Of course I like most of the cowboys. Colin—" Her tongue and lips carressed the name. "Colin is my uncle, they keep saying, but he really isn't, you know. Not by blood. And he's more than a friend. Or he will be. When I grow up a little more—"

Her eyes fell to dreaming, and though I was with part of me afraid of her, I felt increasingly afraid *for* her. Though Colin, whatever his dealings with Anne, didn't seem the kind of man to take advantage of a young girl, even one who was trying so actively and enticingly to seduce him.

For that he deserved some credit, even if I was loath to grant it, for I could imagine to some degree what an appealing temptress such a precocious child could be, physically mature before her emotions could handle what her hungers might provoke.

We had left the narrow trail now and passed over rough terrain studded with rocks, dipping to valleys, all forested. Near a rock slide, I heard a peculiar mewing sound.

"What's that?" I asked.

Cecile glanced up and pointed at a ledge where a pika sat, licking himself like a small cat. "It was that one or a friend. Pikas make all kinds of noises, though. Sometimes they sound like newborn lambs bleating, other times it's more of a bark, or they may squeak like hurt rabbits. Colin thinks different colonies have different dialects, just like people."

Her voice, hard and bright as a diamond ordinarily, always dropped and softened at Colin's name. What a pity that he wasn't her father, or even a real uncle, so that she could have loved him without this dangerous inflection that had to turn him brusque, limit their intimacy.

"They're astonishing little creatures," I said. "Did you ever have one for a pet?"

"They don't do well as captives," Cecile replied, scowling. "Britt kept some in his damned old laboratory and they died."

To my look of horror, she added vindictively, "He won't do that anymore, though. I told him if he did, I'd get him."

"Cecile!"

"I don't care!" she said savagely. "Who does he think he is, shutting wild things up, injecting them with his old messes like a witch doctor? I'd like to give him a nice big shot of his own medicine."

"You'd better not," I said. "He *is* your mother's husband, and besides, you'd probably get shut up yourself."

Shrugging, tossing me a bitter grin, Cecile said, "Why do you think I haven't already done it?"

I couldn't think of anything to say to that. In a few minutes we came over a swell of earth and looked down to a long level stretch, reaching to where the trees began to climb the mountains. There were trees on the tableland, too, lodgepole pine with curious gaps in their foliage girdling the trees at about the same height, leaves below and leaves above, but eaten off for perhaps a foot or two.

Bodies of water gleamed all over the plain. From most of them rose clouds of vapor, while at the far end of the area, dense steam suddenly volleyed up from a miniature volcano, hung in the air several minutes, and ebbed away in gentle snorts as if the cone were breathing.

Could that be Anne's "Suvi"?

Had Cecile brought her to this place that was hard to find, and then one day tripped or shoved her into one of the boiling springs? I could hardly keep from screaming the question for a moment, and I fought to control myself.

Most things, it seemed, were possible at Smoke Valley, but I'd never learn the truth about Anne if I got openly nervous or showed suspicion or fear. Of course I knew that if she had been killed, whoever had done it couldn't scruple to erase me if my identity and purpose were learned.

I looked across the vapored, eerie, beautiful valley, and it seemed to me indeed to be a valley of death. Forcing such thoughts away, striving for normalcy, I walked toward one of the pines.

"What makes them bare at this particular height?" I

asked.

"Moose and elk graze here in the snows." Cecile laughed in a tinkly burst of silver bells. "You should see them, here where the hot vapors keep the air warm, standing about eating off the trees. Like a sauna with a cafeteria!"

I had to laugh at the thought. That would be something to see, when snow shrouded the earth. "I'll try to come often just to watch that," I said.

"Then you'll have to get good on snowshoes or borrow or ride a snowmobile," Cecile said. "I share one with the cowboys. I can take you."

"That's very nice of you," I said, but did not commit myself.

We walked along leached solid earth, stopping at pools of deep emerald green which Cecile told me were colored by algae at one thirty-five to one forty-five degrees, and one of deeper green which she said was a little cooler. A stream ran through the table, orange and red and rusty brown tinting its sides and bottom, these colors caused by variations of heat from ninety to one twenty-five degrees. As we walked, steam swirled off the water to blow on us, warming us until the wind swept it away, or the effusion ebbed. Then I felt cold, not only because of the vanished warmth but because of the damp left on body and clothes.

So in alternating steam heat and mountain chill, we made our way to the edge of the clearing and the belching white-shading-to-pink cone.

As we got closer, I saw the small volcano was larger than it looked from the distance; perhaps fifteen feet high, rising from a whitish mound, with an irregular crater from which the vapor blew at charged intervals before twining mistily away.

When we finally come as near to the cone as discretion allowed, I stared at it with a mixture of fear and marvel. For I was as sure as I could be that this was my sister's favorite, the one she called "Suvi," and I wondered if the girl beside me now had tolled Anne here, the last time fatally.

I felt Cecile's presence vanish. Whirling, I turned. She was gone! Vanished like the vapors that came and went, swelled and disappeared in this beautiful, weird valley.

# 9

The mists swirled away from a rock plateau near the river. For a moment, I saw Cecile before the vapor billowed again between us. I started forward, catching glimpses according to the pulsating, changing flow of steam colored now by the late sun, a sun which gilded the slim nymph body, for Cecile had stripped.

Naked, sun-bright, she swayed and bent and danced as if the rock were an altar and the vapors magic incense of some ancient deity, some spirit of this place.

Pagan, beautiful, altogether strange, beyond the limits of my experience. I stopped perhaps a hundred yards away and watched the girl, charmed, gripped in feelings that were unnameable. She was as much a part of this haunting region as any of its phenomena, and as unexplainable.

She seemed totally unaware of me. There was an absorbed impersonal determination in her face and motions, as if she offered her grace to a god, her only desire to please him. I remembered some snatch of how Hindu dancing girls dance for their gods, in devotion, and how Siva, the Creator-Destroyer, danced old worlds to their end and brought forth new ones with the joy of his moving.

And then, as abruptly as she had slipped away, Cecile strode proudly out of the floating vapors and confronted me, her thin, incredibly lovely straight body poised in flaunting challenge.

"I'll bet you can't do that!" she cried, eyes sparkling.

"No." I was surprised at the sadness in my voice. "No, I can't."

"And you won't even try," she thrust.

"That's right," I said, having to laugh at the very thought of my capering about naked in the steam. "I won't try. On you, it looks good. On me, it would be ridiculous."

She frowned. "How can you know if you haven't tried? You must miss a lot of fun that way."

"Surroundings, I suppose." Amusing, a bit upsetting, for her to quiz me. "There wasn't any place in Missouri to dance like that, and I think if you don't do it before you're a certain age, you never can."

"You could try," she chided.

Her whole body was golden except for the nipples of her small hard breasts, which looked tipped with rouge. Nothing from this child could have surprised me. I felt weighted, awkward, and foolish beside her. Timid, inhibited and *old*, too, though ordinarily I was the one who laughed at proper ceremonies and attitudes, and ordinarily I was the headlong, impulsive tomboy.

"Aren't you cold?" I asked, like a fussy mother.

She smiled and threw back that golden blaze of hair which seemed too heavy for her slender neck. "My blood keeps me warm."

*Tyger, tyger ...*

"You'd better get dressed," I said. "We have to get home. Maybe you can pick your way across that foot log in the dark, but I can't."

Shrugging, she bent for her clothes.

"Cecile!" A distant voice rang out over the valley. "What the devil are you doing?"

We both whirled. Colin McReynolds stood at the other side, too far away to be identified by his face, but it was unmistakably he.

Cecile didn't clutch her things in front of her, but

stood there brazenly, with only an occasional wisp of vapor masking her body. "I've been dancing!" she shouted. "Would you like to see me?"

"Get dressed, young lady, and make it quick!"

She did, and though he was too distant to pick up on the strip-artiste nuances of her sinuous movements, I wasn't. This girl throbbed sex—she knew a lot more about some angles, if not acute and obtuse ones, than I ever would. I could only guess at how sight of her would affect a man, knowing well in his mind she was a child, but surely responding to what his senses telegraphed to those deep core centers that have no intelligence, only drives.

What were her parents thinking of? They might not know how seductive she was around Colin. I had a flash of wondering if I should warn Shana, but the notion turned my stomach. Maybe Tam—? But there were limits to what anyone could do with Cecile. In the long run, Colin must cope with her.

But if he ever slipped, if he ever yielded, I wouldn't be one to blame him much! Especially as she smiled at me and told me, "I knew he was coming here this afternoon."

"And you—danced?"

"Of course," she said merrily. "And he saw me, even if it was a long way off." She sighed. "I don't think most men are like that. Most of them would get a lot closer before they told me to put on my clothes. Britt would."

"He's your stepfather!"

"So? He's no blood kin and neither's Colin."

"Maybe when you're a little older . . ."

She gave me a withering look. "You're older than I am, and what's happened to you?"

What a tongue! I colored hotly. "Precious little as far as men go. But I've got my degree."

"Well, when I'm your age, I won't have a degree but I bet I have a man!" Her gaze fastened to the one who waited with annoyed impatience evident in the very set of his shoulders. "Colin. He's all I want."

Double her age now, but it wouldn't be an unthinkable gap in another four or five years. Somehow that thought gave me a pang, which I assured myself was only horror at Cecile's plotting coolly to get a man at her age, much less implement her plans to some degree.

"How did you know he was coming?" I demanded.

"I told him I was bringing you over to Misty Basin. That's the name of this place." Again she smiled in that superior way that made me want to shake her. "Colin doesn't like me to bring strangers here. Maybe he's afraid I'll shove them in one of the hot pools."

She tripped across the scattered ledges of rock, reaching up to whisper something in Colin's ear with a mischievous glance back at me.

Colin didn't smile. "I'll give you a lift home," he decreed, not offering, just saying what was to be. "It'd be dark by the time you reached that foot log. You know better than to start this walk in the afternoon, Cecy."

"I am Cecile," she rebuked. "And I could walk that log in a storm at midnight."

"Maybe. If you're fool enough to try, it's your neck. But Miss Richardson's a stranger. Come along now. I've got other things to do."

"You don't have to waste your time looking out for me," I said resentfully. "If I fell in the river, I could swim."

"Sure, if you didn't hit your head on a rock or something. Get in the jeep, Miss Richardson. Coming, Cecy?"

She was up and in the middle of the seats in a twinkling. Colin McReynolds gave me a lift up with his big capable hand under my arm, shutting the door emphatically.

We took a rutted, sometimes invisible route back to the main road, jouncing at every breath, for Colin drove as fast as caution allowed, with the skill that comes with long practice. At the fork in the road, he drove toward the ranch.

"Oh, Colin," Cecile wailed. "Don't take me home first."

He didn't say anything but simply continued on, driving faster now that the surface was good.

Cecile caught his arm. "You're mean!" she cried. "You could just as easily take Jan home and then me. You—you like to disappoint me! You—you—"

"Cecy, if you'd act your age, you wouldn't get disappointed," he said, in a rough tone that held, I thought, a note of grim tenderness. "If you'd be the kid you are, the one I taught to ride and swim and tail cows and camp, I wouldn't have to treat you this way. But damn it, somehow, someway, you've decided this last year or so to act like a damned two-bit hooker. And you're not doing that, honey. Not with me!"

Her mouth trembled. "You don't like me anymore."

He kept his eyes on the road and his hands on the wheel, but his voice was so soft that I wondered, with a lurch of my heart, if he didn't feel things for this child, apart from incited lust, that his controls as an adult man wouldn't let him admit.

"Hell, Cecy, when you cut this nonsense, we'll be fine. I care what happens to you. I want you to grow into what you can be. But don't rush, baby. Enjoy your young time now."

"I can't when you freeze me off like this, when you won't be with me alone."

"And I can't be with you alone, you hard-headed brat, till you shape up."

He swung the jeep down the long drive to the incredible English manor house and stopped by the door. I got out to let Cecile climb down sulkily after a last beseeching glance at Colin. We stood near each other for a moment, her eyes almost level with mine, eyes I could not fathom, strange alien eyes in that exotic piquant face framed by its nimbus of radiant hair.

"Can I come tomorrow?" she asked.

"Of course. After lunch?"

She nodded. "If I can't make it then, I'll telephone." Without sparing Colin a look, she walked very straight-backed to the imposing house, vanishing behind its doors.

Colin's mouth was set as he turned the jeep and headed for the main road. "That kid!" he burst out, as if unable to help it. "She used to be so much fun, smart and quick, ready to try anything, brave and sweet. But now—" He shook his head. "I don't know how to handle her."

"It's probably just a stage."

"Well, it started over a year ago, and it's damn sure not getting any better. It was kind of funny at first—she put on her mother's makeup and tried to dress like a siren, and it just looked silly on such a child. But she's dropped that, she's—just herself, she's getting older, and—" His words broke off, and he flexed his hands on the wheel.

"Now it's not funny," I finished for him.

"No. It isn't."

"Have you told Mrs. Lindsay?"

"Anything Shana says to Cecy will only make things worse. Tam won't believe how the little wretch acts because when she's around him, butter wouldn't melt in her mouth, she's our pet baby wrangler again. In fact, Tam half-accused me of being dirty-minded!"

I roared helplessly at that, but sobered abruptly as Colin mused, "Maybe you can straighten her out."

"*Me?*"

"Yup."

I shook my head ruefully. "She may appreciate my helping her with geometry, may even be lonely for someone to talk to, but she has nothing but scornful pity for me otherwise."

"That's not the impression I got from a few remarks she dropped yesterday," Colin said. "Anyway, you don't have to lecture her, boss her around, or create situations where she just naturally has to dig in and rebel." He nodded his head, apparently hopeful of this new solution. "I've always thought that one reasonably normal person around that child would make a great big difference. Paula and the cook love her, but they spoil the hell out of her, which isn't what she needs."

He parked in front of his cabin. "Just a minute. I've got something for you."

Putting his fingers to his lips, he gave a piercing whistle. In a few minutes, four dogs came running, the bigger pair an adult version of the half-grown pups I'd met yesterday. They all frisked forward now, lolloping their tails, curvetting with pleasure, eyes shining, black coats glossy.

"You need a watchdog," Colin said. "You could take just one of the young dogs, but if you can stand it, I wish you'd take the pair. They're inseparable and would be company for each other."

"You're loaning them for the winter?"

His brows raised. "Well, I didn't think you'd want to take them to college or wherever, but if you get attached to them, sure, you can have them at season's end." He grinned. He looked so nice that I wished he weren't always frowning or making like the great stone face. "I'll have to be sure you're a suitable owner, of course, but you don't seem irresponsible."

"You acted before like you thought so, driving out to Misty Basin like that."

His face masked again. "I told you, that foot log is risky after dark."

Tantalized beyond endurance by all the things about Smoke Valley's people that I didn't understand, I made a thrust. "Cecile hinted that you might think she'd push me into one of the boiling streams."

He gave a bark of astonished laughter. "That little kook! She likes to build herself up into something really dangerous. No, I just knew it would be dark when you came back, since you started out so late, and that log is a hazard even in daylight. If you're going to use it, I'll have the men put up a handrail. We do that from time to time, but they always wash out in floods so we don't bother much ordinarily. Very few strangers ever come that way."

But I was sure my sister had.

The dogs still cavorted, clowning, making mock attacks on each other. "Want them both?" Colin asked.

"I'd love to have them!" I said fervently. They would make a big reassuring difference in that creaking lodge at night, let alone providing any real help against intruders. "But won't they miss their parents?"

"They'll be running back and forth," Colin assured me. He whistled the young pair into the back of the jeep and started the motor. "We call them Donner and Blitzen."

I don't know what made me pause in patting the dogs, leaning backwards over the seat, but I did. And as I paused I glanced toward the cabin. A face was at the window.

Shana.

Our eyes locked for a startled second. Then I turned back to the dogs. When I looked sideways again, she was gone. As we jolted off, I wondered what she was doing there, and believed with a kind of sickness that I knew.

If she'd only wanted to see Colin about something, she would have called to him or come out, wouldn't she? And hadn't she developed her incapacitating "headache" at his cabin the afternoon she was to have met me at the airport?

I didn't think that Cecile was alone in her yen for this browned, lean man beside me. How could any man's approach to Shana possibly be Colin's abstemious one with her daughter?

I sat, hands knotted tight in my lap, and wondered why the idea made me miserable. After all, I barely knew him. But he must not have known that Shana was at his cabin, for when he stopped in front of the lodge, he called the dogs inside, produced a bag of dog food and two leashes, and asked in an amusingly plaintive way, "Will you make some coffee?"

"I think I can manage that," I said.

We moved into the kitchen, Donner and Blitzen trotting about sniffing, whisking their tails. "It may take them a while to learn to stay here," Colin said. "If they're hanging around my place at feeding time in the evening, I'll bring them over to you. After they learn that food is here and you've had time to give them some tender loving care, they'll be faithful."

"Just so they're here at night," I said, laughing, trying to cast off the unreasonable depression that glimpsing Shana in his cabin had brought over me. "I certainly will feel a lot safer." But even then it occurred to me that the dogs wouldn't bark at him.

"How do you like the place?" Colin asked, leaning on a counter.

"Very much," I said truthfully. "Of course, it *is* a bit spooky, and I won't be going out in the big hall or upstairs at night. But my bedroom and the kitchen make a nice warm, comfortable area."

"You like the kitchen?"

"Love it! The tiles around the ceiling, the way everything is easy to get at yet not in the way—it's the best kitchen I've ever seen."

Colin nodded. "Glad to hear you say that. I planned the remodeling when the lodge was renovated six years ago."

I gaped in surprise. "I like to cook." he said, half-defiantly. "And I've never been in a kitchen that was right till it had some changes."

"Did you—did you do those water colors in the bedroom?" I asked.

"Yes," he admitted, again defiantly, jaw thrusting forward. "If you don't want them, I'll take them away."

"No, they're lovely!" I protested. "The cook must be a good friend of yours, for you to leave such a collection in the room."

He colored, speaking roughly as if impelled to blurt out the truth quickly. "They're not there while the cook is."

"But then—why—"

"I don't like this idea of girl winter keepers," he said brusquely. "Most of them have no idea how lonely they're going to get. But the country is beautiful, and the animals and birds are fascinating, so I kind of figured that if the keeper got interested in what she can see here, she might not have a bad winter after all." And he looked away as if he had confessed some crime.

"I can't speak for other girls," I said, after a minute. "But I certainly enjoy the pictures and I hope I'll get to see most of the creatures while I'm here."

"Most you probably can," Colin assured. "But some will be hibernating very shortly. I'll—"

Out in the hall, Donner and Blitzen burst into wild barking. Colin and I jumped up, but before we could reach the door, Britt Lindsay stood there, russet eyes playing from one of us to the other, fine-modeled lips curved in a half-smile.

# 10

"How cozy," he said, ignoring the dogs who growled, hackles raised, till hushed by a word from Colin. "A pair of noble canines defending the threshold while you sip coffee in the kitchen. Is there a cup for me?"

I poured him some, cursing the nervousness that made me slosh it over into the saucer. Did he know where his wife was? Did he care? As I gave him the mug, I compared the two men at opposite ends of the counter, hunting for some family likeness.

I found none, except that both were tall, about the same build. Britt had been sketched with a thin-line point and Colin with a blunt one, though there was nothing coarse about him, just a ruggedness. It was the difference between Colin's almost shaggy dun-coyote hair and Britt's silver-burnished locks, shaped as carefully to frame his face as any woman's.

"I suppose he's been telling you about his water colors," Britt went on, with bright malice. "That always gets the ladies—a big silent ranchman's concern for their loneliness and the underlying implication that a strong man who can use a brush with finesse must be adept at other delicate arts."

Colin's face was closed. Denying the sharp pang that Britt's casual barb had caused, I smiled and said, "The pictures are very good. I'm glad to have them in my room."

"Oh, so is every girl," Britt conceded. "Of course, one mustn't take too puritanical a view of it. A single man would have a rough time in Smoke Valley if it weren't for the lodge help in summer and winter keepers the rest of the year."

Did he have any idea at all that his stepdaughter and probably his own wife were hurling themselves at his cousin? Or was he acting like this because he did know?

"Why did you come by?" Colin asked. "Presumably, since you have a wife, you don't share my alleged indiscriminate mania for whoever's living here."

Britt looked annoyed, compressed his lips. "I wanted to be sure Cecile doesn't become a plague with her geometry and other kinks. And I came to tell Jan that Tam's going to Billings tomorrow and that this is her sure chance to lay in supplies of books and whatever before the snows come."

"Cecile is fine," I said, hiding my reservations. "And I'd love to go to town. What time?"

"Tam will stop for you about eight. And Cecile will tag along so you needn't bother to cancel the geometry class."

"Would you get something for me?" Colin asked abruptly.

"If I can find it," I replied.

"Do you still want to fence?"

"Yes."

"Then get me a gauntlet at the sporting shop. The owner's a former collegiate fencing champ—he tried to turn everyone on to it, so he carries a pretty good line."

"Will I need anything?" I asked.

"I've got a mix of rapiers, épées, and sabers, and several padded jackets. What you might want is a smaller mask than those I have."

"May I play?" smiled Britt, a curious light in his eyes. "It's been a long time since we've had a match, Colin. I thought you'd given it up."

Colin ignored the last remark and said quickly, "I've no objection if Miss Richardson doesn't."

"Miss Richardson?" Britt drawled, lifting his fair eyebrows. "My, my! We *are* being genteel. Was it that pretty little Anne Dupree who changed your approach?"

Colin was past me in a second, shoulders stiffly back as if to restrain his hands. "Mention Anne Dupree again and I'll shove your teeth down your throat!"

"My dear fellow," gibed Britt, not giving an inch. "Did you at long last love a girl truly? Does it rankle that she went off with an aging hunter of après-ski orgies?"

Colin put the dogs in the hall and shut the door. Then, moving with deliberation, he slugged his fist into Britt, who staggered back against the wall, lifting his fingers to his mouth, bringing them away bloodied from a cracked lip. Colin's knuckles, too, were marked, as he waited, not pressing the attack but ready.

Slowly Britt straightened. "I look forward to our match," he said to Colin, with a brittle laugh. "You know I don't engage in fisticuffs in your crude provincial way." To me he said, "Thanks for the coffee. Tam will pick you up tomorrow morning."

With a short nod, he turned away, opening the door. The dogs growled after him. Colin gazed as if sightless out the window toward the mountains. My heart was thudding as I tried to think of some way to get information without rousing suspicion. For Britt had confirmed what Cecile had told me, that Colin had been drawn to Anne. And Britt had confirmed her leaving with a man.

"Anne Dupree," I said shakily. "That's an unusual name."

"I suppose." Colin spoke automatically, still lost in whatever he was thinking.

"Cecile said she was very pretty."

"She did?" Colin looked at me now and his eyes, gray and wintry, pierced into me as if searching for whatever I knew.

It took all my will not to glance away and evade that

94

probing stare. Especially since I realized that I was jealous of Anne, of any girl who could cause such obviously strong emotions in this man, who probably didn't even like me, though he might well see me as a pasttime, a fleeting winter sport.

But Anne, I knew, with a pain that arched through my body and turned my stomach numb, had been his love, his summer love, and he remembered her though summer was vanished and so was she.

"What was Cecy telling you about Anne?" he asked, hesitating just a second before her name so that it came out a lingering caress.

"Cecile—" I broke off, not wanting to betray the girl's confidence.

"Yes?" he commanded. His hands closed on my wrists.

My knees went weak, and I could have melted away right then and there. Ridiculous! Stupid! Not to be allowed. Not even if he weren't a prime suspect in the mystery of Anne.

I freed myself. He didn't try to hold me, which of course he could have done almost without exertion, but let his hands drop at his sides in an impotence that stirred my pity. Whatever had happened, he must have loved Anne.

"I don't suppose it matters," he said dully. "Anne drowned. That's all there is to it."

"Are you sure she's dead?"

"What else? Her mother called here and said there'd been a telegram from this jerk she left with. He said she'd been lost while surfing. I guess the body wasn't found, but that's no wonder."

"Did—did you know the man?"

"Just by reputation." Colin's voice was grim. "In spite of what Britt says, I don't hobnob much with the summer people, guests or helpers." His face softened. "Anne was—different."

"She must have been." My mouth felt parched.

Was he telling the truth? It sounded plausible—he didn't strike me as a liar—and yet how much of that was the feeling I could no longer deny he was waking in me?

Oh dreadful, damnable, horrid luck! I was miring down in love—not falling, just sinking, heavily, inevitably, as if caught in quicksand. As much as I feared it, I struggled and seemed to go deeper.

Colin brushed my cheek lightly with his hand. "Good night. Better leash the dogs when you turn them out so they won't trot back to me. In a few days they'll settle here."

"Good night. And thank you."

He nodded and went out.

The dogs whined as he closed the door. I sat down on the floor with them, hugged them, and wept.

The outburst, like a thunder shower, was brief, violent, and cleansed my emotional atmosphere, at least temporarily, of the heavy conflicting currents tangling with each other. I rubbed my eyes, trumpeted into a tissue, and got up and shot the bolt on the door, for dusk was making an opaque curtain outside the windows.

"Come along, fellas," I told the dogs. "Let's see what we can feed you. Donner, you've got the red collar, right? And Blitzen, you're sporting the green number. I suppose Colin named you. I'm glad that at least he stopped short of Cupid and Comet."

My worry that the dogs might refuse food out of loyalty to their master proved totally unfounded. They gobbled up the first lot of dog food I prepared and sat back, tails thumping, eyes expectantly following my every move.

"All right," I said, stirring more warm water into the chunky granules, which exuded what was to me an apalling odor of rancid fish. "But this is it till I check with Colin on how much you should have."

How oddly comforting, in spite of my doubts, to say his name.

I heated soup, made a grilled cheese sandwich, and ate perched on a stool with the dogs settled near me without any noticeable grieving. Something pressed against my side from a pocket, and I reached after it before I remembered and drew it out slowly, cradling it in my palm.

Anne's ring.

How had she lost it? Would we ever know?

My somber thoughts took a horrifying twist. If Anne had gone off with Nordstrom, Colin might have followed them, might have killed her.

But then Nordstrom wouldn't have telegrammed . . .

My relief was overtaken by an undeniable possibility. Colin might have killed them both and sent the telegram in Nordstrom's name. If one body could vanish, why couldn't two?

I attacked the theory, tearing at it frantically to find a contradiction, but it held up. Which didn't mean it was true, only that it could have happened. A man like Colin, deeply in love, thrown over for a feckless playboy type . . . Yes, it might have gone that way. And if it had, everything that Shana had said about Anne's disappearance could be the gospel truth as far as she knew.

Oh, Colin, Colin.

I don't know how long I sat there, but at last the dogs nuzzled me questioningly. I cleaned up the kitchen, slipped on their chain leashes, and took them out, feeling quite safe with the pair of them, though it was difficult when they wanted to go in opposite directions. I solved this by indulging first one and then the other. Colin's cabin showed no light.

Had he gone home to find Shana there? If so, what had happened?

As if in answer, a light suddenly glowed. This time, I didn't find it reassuring or comforting. Though I knew there were all kinds of other feasible explanations for it, I had a swift flash of lovers in the dark, lovers stealing sweetness, and when they were sated, turning on the light.

"Donner!" I called, wheeling sharply, biting my lip. "Blitzen! Hurry up, we can't stay out here all night."

Inside, safely locked up, the dogs curled near my bed

on a large rug, I wrote mother about Cecile's geometry and Misty Basin and the watch dogs, things that ought to make her feel I was enjoying the place and not getting lonely. But I didn't feel able to tell her about the people or the convoluted web spun by their relationships in which Anne, to some degree, must have been entangled.

The more I turned over such facts as seemed supported, the more fresh intricacies and suspicions cropped up. If Shana loved Colin, or even felt simply physical possessiveness for him, couldn't she have disposed of her rival? Or had a hand in it?

I buried my head in my hands, trying to calm the throbbing. Only one thing was sure. I could trust no one near the focal point of my sister's disappearance. I must be on guard, always. Why, even these dogs Colin had given me wouldn't warn me of him or protect me against him, as he knew very well.

It was a long time that night before I slept.


I woke with a sharp notion in my mind, and held it as I dressed quickly and ate breakfast, for I had slept past seven after drowsing only fitfully until the wee hours.

Had Colin gone to California during the time Anne was supposed to be there? It shouldn't be impossible to find out. If he hadn't been there, the hateful suspicion that tormented me could be hushed. Though of course I couldn't yet discard the idea that Anne had died here in Smoke Valley and the California drowning was an ingenious ruse.

I was just about ready when a dark green pickup wheeled into the clearing. I caught up my purse and coat, unbolted the door, and opened it to find Tam climbing up the steps. Not he, a honker of horns for women!

"Mornin'." His walnut-lined wrinkled face broke into a pleased grin. "And you look bright as the dawn, ma'am! Got your shopping list and all?"

"Yes, thanks. It's good of you to take me."

"A pleasure, ma'am." He put his hand under my elbow to help me down the stairs, then went around and opened my side of the pickup. "All the young pup hands wanted to take you, but I pulled my seniority."

Cecile was in the middle seat.

"Glad to see me?" she teased. "Or sorry?"

"Did you bring your geometry?" I parried, clambering up.

The truth was, I had been looking forward to a chance to question Tam, to find out whatever he could tell me, especially since he'd be going to the north range soon and I might not see him again. But I consoled myself with the hope that the two of them chatting together might drop information that I wouldn't have the knowledge to ferret out.

"Britt says that you're going to fence with Colin," Cecile said, like a child pointing out that she hadn't been invited to a party. "I want to learn. You will let me, won't you?"

"Why, of course," I said. "But Britt is coming, too, at least for one match."

"I hope Colin slashes him," she said vindictively.

"Cecile, the object of fencing is not to wound. The weapons have rubber tips, and a touch on the opponent should be light. Besides, there are target areas, and a touch beyond these is a foul except in épée, where any touch counts."

She made a mocking face, green eyes dancing. "You *are* a born teacher, aren't you, Jan? I'll bet you give your boyfriends instructions on how to kiss."

"I don't pretend to know much about that," I said, trying to conceal the sting her remark had left. "But if you want to fence, it has to be by the rules. Otherwise it's dangerous."

"Good!" she said.

I didn't know whether or not Tam could hear us, but he cut in firmly, putting his gnarled hand on her jeans-covered knee in an admonitory gesture she didn't try to escape.

"Now, listen, Cecy girl, if you're going to learn this sword business, you learn it right. None of your tricks! I heard Colin tell you you could come if Miss Jan agreed, but you promised him there'd be no foolishness. Now you promise me, or by gum, we aren't buying your gol-durned equipment. And when Colin wants to know why, I'll tell him."

"Oh, Tam! You wouldn't be so mean."

"Mean, nothin'. Your mama doesn't know what to do with you—somebody's got to!"

She pouted. "I wouldn't *really* hurt Britt."

"Well, he might hurt you, silly! Ever stop to think about that? He's a good fencer, Colin says, and God knows he doesn't like you any better than you like him."

"That's so," the girl assented.

"Promise?" demanded Tam.

She gave a long sigh, giggled, and squeezed his hand, touching it to her cheek before guiding it back to the wheel. "All right, blackmailer. I promise. But," she added doggedly, "Britt's going to get his someday, and I want to see it happen."

"If you ask me," Tam said drily, "he paid for all his sins when he got you for a stepdaughter! Why don't you just keep clear of him, Cecy?"

"I do, mostly." Her eyes darkened to deep emerald. "But he's still there."

"It's his ranch," Tam reminded her.

"He's got no more right to it than Colin. Actually, not as much, because Colin works, keeps things going."

"If Colin's satisfied, why should you kick?" Tam countered. "He'll inherit the place anyway if Britt doesn't have children, and that doesn't seem likely anymore."

"Britt could outlive Colin," Cecile argued. "And what's the good of getting something when you're too old to care?"

Tam cackled and gave her an affectionate rallying glance, while the pickup meandered alarmingly to the wrong side of the road. "Honey, as long as you're livin', you always care!"

Noticing simultaneously my look of fright and the drift of the pickup, he righted it, grumbling, "Dang contraption's got no sense! Go anywhere. Just like a chicken with its head off. Now a good horse, he'll just pick out the way once you point him. And he'll keep going when he's out of gas, too, he'll run on heart, till it busts. But these suckers—"

The rest of the way to Billings, he talked about the old days while Cecile warned him of crossroads and when he had to stop. They had a system worked out whereby she raised her hand when all was clear and touched his arm when he ought to stop. She was a different person with him, like a granddaughter, and he plainly doted on her, though he'd straighten her out ruthlessly for her own good.

Tam's stories were epic history, the bitter struggles between ranchmen and farmers, in which his father had apparently hung and shot a good many men, as well as being at the hanging of Cattle Kate down in Wyoming—pretty, wild Kate who had loved too many men and branded too many cattle belonging to other people.

Tam himself had seen some colorful days. He laughed as he told how he once fell in on the trail with an Arkansan possessed of the old "wild, woolly and full of fleas, hard to curry below the knees" braggadocio. It didn't take them long to quarrel, and Tam had gestured contemptuously at the Arkansan's pearl-handled revolver.

"You take first shot," he'd said. "When they find your carcass, I want your gun dirty."

The Arkansan decided his route lay in another direction. Tam chortled to remember, and then told how, when sheep were proving thriftier and surer money than cattle, and had at last been accepted by cattlemen, he had gone into raising his own flock on land his father leased from Britt's grandfather.

"One way sheep and hogs are alike," Tam explained. "They crowd in to feed and shove out the weak or timid ones, who just plain starve if the man raisin' them don't have any sense. But I studied it, hit on moving the shy or runty ones down to another lot and feeding place, and then moving the runtiest out of that to another feed lot till all of them were getting nice and fat." He chuckled at the memory. "I lost fewer sheep and got the highest prices of any man in the whole state! So then they reckoned I wasn't so dumb, taking a little pains with my stock."

It was an education, listening to him. His ears and eyes might not be so sharp anymore, but his mind was keen and honed as an old premium-quality knife, nicked and worn but far superior to brand-new mass-produced ones.

Once in Billings, we parked by the sporting goods shop and Cecile and I agreed to meet Tam for lunch at one, when we could see how much we had left to do. The owner of the shop greeted Cecile warmly and helped us fit masks. Cecile ordered from his catalog a complete fencing outfit, except for a white tunic he had in stock which fitted her, ignoring his suggestion that she wait to see whether she liked the sport.

"I shall become very good at it," she told him in a matter-of-fact way. "Because it is Colin's favorite thing of this sort."

"He used to be excellent," the man said. "Glad you're getting a little club going up there. Britt Lindsay was a great fencer, too, especially with saber, but—" He broke off, turning to the counter.

"But what?" demanded Cecile.

"Oh, some people get carried away in a match," said the balding, still trim man. "Anything else, ladies?"

I got Colin's gauntlet and rubberized high boots, paid for my own mask, and charged everything else as Tam had instructed me to. Next we made it to a hobby shop, where I got crewel materials and Cecile bought a bead loom. She skipped the bookstore, and while I was absorbed there, wishing I had enough money to buy hundreds of books instead of what I could afford, she went to a drugstore for what she called "beauty needs."

It was all done by the time we met Tam at a

steakhouse, so after thick juicy steaks and crisp salad, we started home.

Tam dropped me at the lodge in late afternoon, jumping out and coming around to help me carry in my purchases, plus a mysterious-looking package he gave me after we had put the other things down.

"Something you'll need this winter," he said. "Wear them in luck!" He put out his hand. "Colin can show you how to use those. And he's a fine young man, even if I am kind of prejudiced, having raised him after his ma went East to get married and respectable. If I don't see you again, ma'am, I surely wish you well." He paused, considered me, and added softly, "You'll find the winter beautiful if you don't let it scare you and use your head."

We shook hands, but that wasn't enough. I bent forward and kissed his cheek, too. "Thank you," I said, eyes moist at his kindness. "It was wonderful to hear you talk today. And if I can somehow, I'll get up to your winter quarters." I was already planning to take him a cake or something nice.

"Smile pretty at Colin and he'll bring you in one of the snowmobiles," Tam joked. His face sobered and he lowered his tone, though Cecile was still in the pickup. "Snowmobiles can be dangerous, ma'am. If I were you, I wouldn't ride much with anyone but Colin."

Before I could ask why, he waved and was gone.

# 11

Tam's gift was snowshoes, reminding me rather of streamlined, graceful tennis rackets, about three-and-a-half feet long and perhaps fifteen inches wide. I hadn't thought about needing them; however, I certainly didn't intend to be trapped inside while the world glittered and gleamed in ice and snow, and what I'd heard about snowmobiles made them seem less and less like anything I'd try running by myself, even if I were permitted the occasional use of one.

Donner and Blitzen were not at the lodge, and I concluded that they had gone back to Colin, which meant that he'd bring them back tonight. I put his fencing gauntlet out where I'd be sure to remember to give it to him and carried my books and crewel supplies to my room.

The bookshelves soon looked comfortingly full for long winter evenings, and the crewel materials fitted nicely into an Indian fiber basket done in natural green, cream, and brown colors. Placed by the big chair, the needlework gave an air of homelike permanence, of productive, if solitary, hours.

Hanging the snowshoes on a hook by the door exhausted my present means of personalizing the room, but it did now seem mine. At least I didn't have that vaguely uneasy sense of being an intruder. I stood in the entrance, surveying the effect, highly pleased.

Next time I went walking, I'd gather some dried grasses and pods and plants to make a winter bouquet, and when Donner and Blitzen were curled up on the rug, this would be home, no matter how the winds blew or how deep the snow piled up outside.

I felt rather than heard someone behind me, whirled around to find Britt Lindsay less than a hand's breadth away so that my body brushed his. I stepped back quickly.

"Don't jump out of your skin," he mocked laughingly. "It's such a pretty covering!"

"I'm not used to people coming up on me like that," I retorted sharply. "Why didn't you knock or call or something?"

"I did knock. You must not have heard. And then when I saw you looking so happy about something, curiosity prevailed."

His pale sherry-colored eyes strayed over my face but stopped before they could travel lower, as if he knew that I was annoyed at him and suggestive behavior on his part would turn me really hostile. He glanced instead at the books, the needlework, raising an eyebrow at the snowshoes.

"You intend to go floundering though the drifts, my dear?"

"I certainly won't stay inside all the time."

"No, but— Well, I hope you won't go far by yourself. Storms can come up suddenly, or you might slip and get an injury that would strand you till it was too late for help."

"I'll be careful, naturally," I replied.

His eyes came back to me. "Ah. Are you naturally careful? Always?" This time his gaze slipped to my throat, where the pulse was hammering so hard I knew he must see it. Though I didn't like him, his presence was physically disturbing and, experienced as he was, he must read this. That knowledge made me feel trapped, vulnerable.

"I try," I said, more loudly than necessary.

"What a pity," he said softly. "One misses so much that way. Still—" He shrugged and looked again at the snowshoes, then turned on me with a burst of teasing laughter. "You're lying!" he said. "You're not careful! Your even taking this job proves that! And a cautious woman, my child, does not go mushing about alone on snowshoes in her first Montana winter."

"I don't know what the rest of this discussion is about," came a voice from the hall. "But I'd agree with that last statement." Preceded by Donner and Blitzen, Colin strode into the kitchen.

"Give him the lecture," said Britt, indicating Colin with gay malice in his eyes.

"What lecture?" asked Colin.

"Jan's views on knocking or shouting before entering the lodge," explained Britt gravely.

"Colin has to bring the dogs home," I flashed. "It's entirely different be—"

"Because it's he?" gibed Britt, and muscles corded in his jaw as he stared at his cousin.

"The door was open and I heard voices," Colin said. "Otherwise, I would have knocked." His gray eyes dwelled on me only a second before he ended formally, "Forgive the intrusion."

Did he think I was carrying on something with Britt? At that moment, I could have cheerfully kicked the owner of Smoke Valley, especially when Colin said, "Well, Jan, here are your dogs. I'll be going."

"Oh, no!" I burst out involuntarily, shaken at the thought of being left alone with Britt, and also, to a degree I was not yet ready to admit, unwilling to have such a short glimpse of Colin. "Wouldn't you like some coffee?"

"Love it," said Britt, easing onto a kitchen stool.

I gave Colin a mutely imploring glance which he answered with a puzzled frown. "Some coffee would taste good," he said, almost dubiously.

So I put coffee on to percolate, fed and patted the black dogs, gave them fresh water, and then, after washing, got out a plate of nut bread and three coffee mugs.

Both men were silent, so while we had coffee I found myself chatting with undue animation about the trip to Billings and the old-time stories Tam had recounted.

"The Wild West saga," yawned Britt. He touched the fencing mask on the table. "When are we having a match, Colin?"

"Tomorrow night?"

"Fine. Where?"

Colin looked at me. "The main hall of the lodge would be the best place. Is that all right with you, Jan? You're going to fence, aren't you?"

"I want to. And Cecile bought a mask today, she wants to learn."

Neither man spoke for a moment. Then Britt laughed harshly. "Well now! If Shana will join in, we'll have full enrollment."

"Then how about eight o'clock?" suggested Colin. "We can store our gear in the lodge and save dragging it back and forth."

Britt nodded and stretched, flexing himself. It was strange that two men who were about the same size should look so different. Britt had a sort of narrow, elusive stance, like an elongated shadow in eclipse, while there was something very solid and substantial about Colin.

"It'll be good exercise, fencing," Britt said. "I haven't fenced since I got tossed off the collegiate team."

"For fouling, wasn't it?" asked Colin.

"The point slipped," shrugged Britt.

Colin gave him a thin look. "Well, we need to be sure all the weapons are securely tipped." He grinned at me. "Looks like you're going to have plenty of company these winter nights!"

"I'll be glad of it," I returned honestly. Not only for people to remind me I was part of a human world, but also because they were the keys to whatever had become of Anne. "I hope Shana will come," I added, thinking in this vein, with the sense of being an intriguer, a spy, both hateful and exciting.

I didn't really want to know that any of these people, or a combination of them, had conspired in a lie about my sister. However it had happened, she was dead. And since Colin seemed the most highly motivated suspect, I found I was hoping more and more, though with a feeling of guilt toward Anne—sweet, lovely, childish Anne who should have loved and laughed in the sunlight for many many years—that she had died as Nordstrom had reported, in a surfing accident during an escapade with him.

But however much I might want Colin to be innocent, I had to remember that he might have done murder, perhaps even two; and if he had, Shana might be an accomplice in covering up the truth, probably out of passion for him.

If they knew I was Anne's sister ...

I shivered a little and bent to pat Donner in order to conceal it, to hide my face till I had my feelings under control. Britt touched Donner—distinguished so far, for me, from Blitzen only by his red collar—who gave a deep warning growl.

"You're leaving these half-grown characters with Jan for protection?" Britt asked jeeringly. "A lot of good they'll be to her!"

"They barked at you," Colin said lightly. "And they'd put up a good tussle if anyone broke in, give Jan a chance to get out or phone for help. Of course, mostly they're for company."

Britt smiled at me. "If you'd like a dog," he offered, "let me give you something better than these pups. We have a neighbor who raises Russian wolfhounds, and he's got a couple he's ready to sell. Now there you'd really have a dog!"

Kneeling between the big pups, I put a hand on each protectively. "Thank you, but I like these!"

"They're Colin's, you know," Britt warned softly. "They'll always be his first and yours second." His mouth jerked down at the corner, showing his even, very white teeth. "Suppose—no offense, Colin, old man—but suppose *he* broke in?"

"I already thought of that," I retorted, evoking a shocked glance from Colin and a wondering frown from Britt. "But that's hardly apt to happen. And I like Donner and Blitzen."

"The foolish virgin," murmured Britt. "All right, have fun with those canine Rover boys. See you tomorrow night." But he didn't leave. He waited for Colin, who gave each dog a pat and soft word before he told me good night, his face unreadable.

The two tall men went out together. I bolted the door and walked quickly through the shadowy vast hall to the familiar warmth of the kitchen.

Cecile was giddy the next day, wound up about fencing that night. When I asked if she'd like me to teach her how to stand and a few basics, she shook her bright head till the curls bounced.

"Thanks, Jan, but Colin's going to teach me! He said he would!" The shine in her eyes became a glint as she added glumly, "I just wish Mother and Britt weren't coming."

"Oh, is your mother going to fence?" I asked, with an absurd sinking of my own heart.

"When she heard Colin was, she decided it was just what she needed for exercise," said Cecile spitefully. "Of course, she *hates* exercise. The only thing I've ever heard her say she enjoyed was riding to hounds in England—chasing down some poor little fox." Then Cecile had a cheering thought, and gave a small wicked laugh. "She can't stand to be awkward, though, or look anything except perfect. If she has trouble learning, maybe she'll drop the whole idea."

Looking at Cecile, I was positive that if she could make her mother seem ludicrous, she would. In a way, I echoed the wish that Shana, lithe and exquisite, perhaps already Colin's lover, wouldn't be present at the fencing, but on another, deeper level I knew the more I saw of Shana, the likelier I was to discover the truth about Anne.

Geometry was a total loss that day. If I hadn't been strung up myself, I might have soothed and guided Cecile, but it was beyond me, so when Cecile finally snapped her book shut and plaintively suggested a walk, I was content to agree.

"This weather can't last much longer," she said, as we swung along, going in a new direction this time, into the forest on the west. "But at least you can still see some of the flowers. You really ought to stay through the summer. Places are thick with evening primroses, windflowers, columbines, wild roses—oh, dozens and dozens of kinds. And monkey flowers! Sort of like snapdragons. Big yellow ones grow around the warm springs, but a deep-red kind blooms along cold streams, and some yellow ones can grow in run-offs from geysers, in water hotter than you'd like to bathe in."

"Is there poison ivy?" I asked gingerly.

"Almost none, but there are plenty of wild berries and grapes. We came this way because we may still find some fringed gentian."

"Is that it?" I asked, pointing to a clump of lavender blooms some distance away.

"Those are asters," my guide said, with a glance of compassion for my ignorance. "They can be purple and blue, almost white."

She pointed out a wild rose briar with beautiful autumn foliage, a red-limbed sort of dogwood that bore white berries, and she bent to touch the flame-colored leaves of the geranium, which had lost its flowers but kept its color.

We passed one stretch where a fire must have cleared the trees, for bits of charred log dotted the area. But plants as tall as Cecile ranged over the ravaged land, an unbelievable blaze of red leaf.

"Fireweed," Cecile dismissed it casually. "It grows best where there's been a fire, and in season its flowers are a deep purply rose."

And then we were on the verge of a kind of natural amphitheater, a rough half-circle of rocks spilling from the foothills, almost surrounding a thick-grassed open glade.

"This is a good place to watch elk and deer," Cecile told me, sharing her knowledge expansively, flattered by my genuine interest. "I've even seen a grizzly here."

I looked about apprehensively, and she laughed. "They can weigh up to five and six hundred pounds, rip a man open with one swipe of their claws. But mostly bears that haven't been bothered by people aren't mean. They eat their berries and lily bulbs, grubs and ants, and seldom prey on anything bigger than squirrels. You probably won't see any bears, they're all going to sleep for winter." Her face darkened "Britt tried to trap one last year for his experiments. I sprayed repellent over every trap he put out. He never did know why he didn't catch his bear!"

Remembering the wire cages in Britt's laboratory, I nodded heartily. "I'm glad you were able to stop it."

"Even if I didn't like bears, I'd be glad to jam his wheels," the girl said. Shrugging, she laughed with delight at the rich blue purple flowers scattered about the clearing. "We're in time! See the gentians? No other flower at all has quite that same fabulous shade."

I moved forward, careful not to tread on any of the spired plants, kneeling on the springy thick grass to examine the little individual blossoms. The petals had a wonderful glowing texture, as if they knew that winter would take them soon and they must concentrate all their life in this hauntingly brilliant late blooming.

"They are beautiful," I said reverently. "Thank you, Cecile. To think that I'd almost surely would have missed them otherwise!"

"Oh, I can show you lots of things," she said loftily. "Tam and Colin know Smoke Valley better than anyone, and they've taught me."

"So that makes you third?"

"Second." Her voice deepened with regret. "Tam can't see or hear so well anymore."

We started back for the lodge, but I looked back after a few minutes, catching my breath in delight. An elk, heavy antlers spreading so wide it seemed they must weigh him down, had appeared at the far edge of the meadow.

"He's an old one," Cecile remarked, after a calculating squint. "Those antlers must be five feet across. Can you see his mane?"

I thought I could distinguish a dark fringe against the brownish neck, which was darker than the rest of the animal. "He's putting on his winter coat," Cecile explained. "The summer red-brown's changing to brownish-gray, but his rump-patch will stay yellow, and he's got a white tail. Sometimes you can see a hundred or so of them together."

I gasped, trying to imagine that. "What a country!" I breathed.

Cecile nodded. "I love it. If I didn't, I'd run off."

"Where?"

"Back to Jamaica." She flourished her arms and did a gliding whirl that sent the image of her dancing naked in Misty Basin flashing through my mind. "Back to my black daddy. My father is black, you know. That's why Britt wouldn't adopt me, even if I'd let him."

I didn't know what was the tactful thing to say, but it seemed wrong to ignore the information she'd vouchsafed. "Do you remember your father, Cecile?"

"No," she said abruptly, and walked ahead of me so fast I thought it best not to catch up.

# 12

About sundown that day, Colin brought Donner and Blitzen to the lodge for feeding. He then marked out the fencing strips with chalk on the hall floor. He also had brought all the fencing equipment, and by the time we'd put it out for easy selection—masks, jackets, épées, sabers, and foils with Italian, French, or Belgian grips—it was so late I invited him to stay and have some of the stew I had simmering for dinner.

With bread and cheese and butter, it made a satisfying meal, and I was glad I had bothered to put in a bay leaf and oregano, basil and thyme, which brought out the tomato and beef taste, mingling deliciously with onions, carrots, and a few potatoes. I like stew about half meat, half vegetable, with just enough rich thick juice to prove the marriage of flavors a success. Apparently Colin did, too, for after a second bowl, he sighed contentedly and practically beamed at me in a way I wouldn't have believed possible.

"Say, that was great! You could get a job cooking any old day."

"Don't say that after one trial," I laughed. "There are thousands of things I've never even tried to make, but I have several pretty foolproof standbys."

"Anyone who worked out those seasonings is a born

cook," he insisted. "But if you want to convince me further, I'll gladly judge any other efforts!"

"Well, when you're by at mealtime, you can always try your luck, but half the time you'll get odds and ends."

"Fair warning," he nodded, gazing wistfully at the orange kettle that held the rest of the stew. "If we weren't fencing in an hour, I'd be a pig and ask for a third bowl."

"Take a container home with you," I suggested, and ladled most of what was left into a plastic refrigerator box. "You can get this before you leave."

"I'll remember!" Colin vowed.

He slid off the stool and began washing dishes while I put the food away. It was highly domestic, the shared meal creating a warm feeling of home. I felt ridiculously happy and exhilarated, feeling a peculiar peaceful unspoken communication with this big, gray-eyed man unlike anything I'd ever experienced.

*But he had loved Anne,* I reminded myself sharply, fighting the euphoric sensation that battered against the walls of doubt and fear. *And he may have killed her—don't be a fool! Even if he had nothing to do with her disappearance, he may not be interested in you, silly! He's enjoyed a good meal, that's all, and those vibrations you're getting are gratified hunger pangs.*

These admonitions failed to suppress a melting in my knees when his hand brushed mine as we reached for the same dish, but if he felt anything, he did a masterly job of concealment, and I thought morosely that it wasn't fair for me to be this overwrought if he was immune.

He hung up the dish towel with an air of that's-that, turned to me, and dropped his hands to my shoulders in a way that wasn't grasping yet left me utterly unable to move. He watched me for a moment, smiled slowly, and touched my cheek very lightly with his fingertips before he cradled my face and put his mouth on mine.

Indescribable. Every kiss, every groping student romance I'd ever struggled through, ceased to exist or form any standard of reference. Only a sudden memory of Anne—a vision of her staring at me with stricken eyes the way she had when we'd quarreled as children and I'd hurt her—made me stiffen in Colin's arms and try to move  back.

He didn't, for even a moment, force me. His hands fell to his sides. "Sorry." His eyes searched mine and he frowned. "Jan, you can't believe that nonsense Britt was telling you? About my giving all the lodge staff girls a tumble?"

"It's none of my business if you do," I said tightly. "Except when it might seem to be my turn."

Colin stood as if wondering whether to continue, looking so thoroughly miserable that I lacerated myself. But the fact of Anne remained. Maybe he didn't romance many girls from the lodge, or give every winter keeper a heavy rush, but the evidence was strong that he had courted my sister.

Not that I blamed him for that—but what if he had killed her? Till I knew he hadn't, it was best to let him think my reserve was caused by Britt's malicious insinuations.

So I made my voice bright and flippant, though I was crying inside. "I guess, Colin, that I don't care for seasonal flings."

"Neither do I," he said grimly. "Neither do I!"

Before I could move, he caught me, and this time there was nothing gentle in his kiss. Gone was wooing, lightness, tentative exploration. This kiss was hard and fierce as his arms, shattering, breaking down defenses, leaving me blind and dizzy.

When he let me go at last, I almost fell, and he didn't steady me. "I won't do that again till you ask me," he said as I leaned against the counter. "If you aren't scared of loving, if you're not an abject coward, you'll give us a chance, let yourself know me."

While I stood by the counter, unable to move or speak, he let his eyes touch my face a last lingering moment before he turned, striding down the hall. I heard him moving furniture in the front of the lodge, but I went to my room and didn't venture out till I heard a motor cut off outside, and voices on the porch.

Cecile had on her white tunic, smartly buttoned at the shoulder and down one side. Britt also wore a tunic with a red patch over the heart. Shana had on beige stretch pants and a high-necked ski sweater. Her hair was coiled round in a sinuous knot at the nape of her neck, secured with sandalwood pins, intricately carved on the top. Cecile gave me a wide grin and sped over to Colin, who was marking more chalk lines on the floor.

Shana held out her hand in greeting. "Hello, Jan. I hope you don't mind a spectator?"

"Not a bit, you can help referee!" I laughed.

Britt examined all of the weapons leaning in the corner, then finally handed me a saber. "This seems the best of a not too good conglomeration," he remarked.

"Thanks," I said, putting the saber down while I selected one of the ungainly padded practice jackets, buckled it on, and picked up a foil with an Italian handle. "But I think I need a match with the foil before trying the saber."

"Ladies' choice," smiled Britt. "Will you fence Colin or me?"

"Why not me?" cried Cecile, planting herself in front of me.

"Because you need some lessons first, you young heathen," cut in Colin. "And I shall give them to you. So come down here, Cecy, and Britt and Jan can have a go while I show you the basics."

It was probably better for the girl not to be taught by her grudging stepfather, but I very shortly found myself wishing I weren't fencing with him, either. He had frightening speed, and an uncanny skill at the straight thrust. He was half into his attack several times before I even knew it.

Perhaps the most unnerving thing was that his well-shaped lips never lost their smile beneath the wire mask.

Of course, at school I had fenced mostly with girls, but I had had male instructors. None of them had ever affected me as Britt did. He pressed his attack, giving me no chance to collect myself, and had scored the required five touches when Colin's voice came from the side.

"I think I'd better referee. Cecy, watch, and see how they go at it."

Fortified by Colin's presence, I was able to salute and start a new match. We went through several phrases—exchanges of movement that passed attack back and forth—before Britt attacked in *octave,* low outside.

I dropped my point in a half arc and riposted under Britt's arm to touch his chest.

Cecile clapped, Shana laughed, Colin called out the score. That was my first and last taste of glory. Britt pressed me harder than ever, making me retreat to the boundaries, and when I counterattacked, he scored at once with a stop thrust, showing himself a master of riposte and parry. He then touched me four times quickly, and as I parried a new attack by overprotecting, moving my foil too far to the side, he disengaged, passing his point under my wrist, and scored the winning touch.

Winded, absolutely humiliated, I started to take off my mask, but Colin said, "Are you too tired for a bout with me, Jan?"

I was, but I wouldn't say so. "Just let me get a drink," I said, and took my time going to the kitchen where I rinsed my mouth and took a few slow sips.

Did Colin want to battle me down, too? He had more reason than Britt. When I came back, he was fencing with Shana, who got her foil knocked from her hand, apparently not for the first time, and flung away in disgust as I approached.

"It's a sport for schoolgirls!" she huffed, and sat down while Cecile gloated.

Colin and I saluted, went into the on guard position. I attacked boldly in *sixte,* deciding I might as well get the agony over with. Colin parried. I disengaged my blade, dropping it to *quarte,* but Colin brought his point under and around my blade, placing it back in *sixte,* and thrusting to score.

He had worked for it, though. This was the "conversation with steel," the mixture of chess and action that fencing, at its most pleasurably challenging, could be.

I grinned, relaxed my grip on the handle a second, tightened thumb and first finger to control the blade, and advanced a few steps before I fell back, inviting Colin's attack. I lunged forward into his advance and touched.

"Bravo!" he called.

My nerve and confidence came back. He fenced more aggressively, and we had an exciting match that made me perform beyond my usual best.

He defeated me five-three, but I was certainly not ashamed of my showing. We shook hands and Colin smiled. "Why don't you take Cecy to the other end and show her the parries?" he asked. "I think it's time Britt and I had the sabers."

Britt's fox eyes sparkled. "You're rash, cousin," he said. "Remember, while you were fencing college oafs, I was training in Europe with Hungarian champions!"

"Can't say that worries me," grinned Colin.

They saluted, and though I was obediently trying to show Cecile the parries in *sixte, quarte, octave,* and *septime,* it was pretty hopeless. She was unable to tear her eyes away from the men in that narrow field of battle, and soon, neither could I.

Each man had his left fist brought down on his hip, out of the way of cuts, for the whole body above the lower stomach was target area. They stood in *tierce,* sabers about the level of the lower outside hip, points directed at the opponent's eyes.

Britt lunged first, lowering his point while thrusting his arm forward. Colin's blade obstructed the attack. Britt "beat" Colin's blade, striking it sharply, and scored.

Both returned to on guard. Colin turned the edge of

his blade, stretching his arm to Britt's head. Britt parried but left the top of his mask exposed so that Colin scored.

Watching them was beautiful. They moved in a violent, close-timed dance. Both could *fleche*—put themselves in full run to attack—but Britt was more prone to this dangerous tactic than Colin and was touched twice while launching himself on his opponent. Both were expert at feinting.

Britt feinted for the head, rotated his forearm, and cut Colin's flank. Next, Colin scored a tempo cut on Britt's head during Britt's preparation to attack. Britt scored again with a head feint and chest cut, but Colin made the winning cut by a *fleche* that brought him by Britt's left, feinting to the head, and as Britt parried, twisting hand and forearm to the right, cutting Britt's flank.

The contest was finished. But as Colin relaxed, dropping his left hand which had been behind him during the bout, Britt lunged suddenly, slashing with the edge of his saber against the unprotected hand.

Colin caught his opponent's sword wrist. "Britt, damn you! The match was over!" He shoved the slighter man away, hard, so that Britt skidded against the wall and stood there, chest heaving, seeming for a moment almost demented.

Cecile had run forward at her stepfather's attack. Now she seized Colin's hand, raising it gently. I was close behind and could see the ugly welt rising across the back of the hand, bloody at one end where the blunted saber had struck with enough force to tear flesh.

"Can you move it?" I asked, trying his fingers one by one.

He reclaimed his hand from both Cecile and me. "Nothing seems to be broken," he said. "Guess you just got carried away, Britt. Can happen."

"Don't be such a damned good guy," Britt steamed. "I'm out of practice! You knew that, and I'll bet you've been getting ready for tonight a long time, haven't you, you—you bastard?"

Colin just looked at him while blood trickled from his hand, falling in bright droplets to the floor. "If you think I'll leave Smoke Valley for a name, Britt, guess again. And if you'll come outside, I'll take pleasure in beating hell out of you, even with a bad hand."

"I don't brawl."

"If you foul me again, by word or saber, you'll brawl or take a beating," Colin said. "Remember that."

He held Britt's eyes till those of Smoke Valley's owner dropped. Then Colin ruffled Cecile's hair. "It's okay, kid. Put on your mask, and I'll show you a few parries."

But Shana, who hadn't moved during Britt's assault and the verbal exchange, came up beside Colin, her eyes unseeing, and touched the blood on his hand.

"Shana!" Britt cried.

Her eyes dilated. She flinched, staring at the blood on her fingers, and raised them to her face so that a red streak appeared there. Her expression was an echo of that girl of the portrait who stared at the fox's brush in a trance of horror.

Britt pushed Cecile away and seized his wife's arm. "What's wrong with you?" he shouted, giving her a shake. "You—are you crazy? Getting his blood on you like a—a savage?"

He picked up her jacket and shoved her into it. "We're going," he snapped. "Cecile, are you coming now?"

"I'll bring her," Colin said tightly. "No point in ruining her evening."

Britt's gaze flickered to me. "I would have thought you'd want the girl out of your way, cousin. But then, your methods are devious, aren't they?" He nodded to me. "Sorry for the furor, Jan. Sometime you and I must have a nice quiet match of our own without all this interference. You're quite good, you know. Just need to develop a bit of dash."

He maneuvered Shana out while the three of us who

remained glanced at each other, spirits heavy, the atmosphere tangled and full of threat, currents that I, at least, didn't understand.

"The only dash I'll have with him is away from him!" I said fervently. "He's out for blood."

"He only got a little," Colin shrugged, wiping off his hand and blotting up the floor.

"Do you have antiseptic and tape?" Cecile demanded. "Come to the kitchen and let me take care of your hand, Colin."

"It's all right."

"You wouldn't say that if it had happened to anyone else!" she retorted, and grasping his good hand, she urged him down the hall. I followed, thoroughly bemused, and hunted out antiseptic, cotton balls, gauze, adhesive tape, and scissors.

"Good grief, ladies!" scoffed Colin.

He took the antiseptic, doused his hand, and refused further ministrations. "It'll heal faster in the air and I've got my tetanus shots," he said. "Now, Cecy, if you're to learn anything tonight except how adults can act like fools, we'd better get with it."

# 13

They left after forty minutes, in which Cecile showed promise of making an excellent fencer. She was lithe, shrewd, and alert, difficult to confuse even at this early stage, a born combatant, whereas I had always had to remind myself the foils were tipped and no one would get hurt, that the foil or saber could not wound.

Unless someone fouled, as Britt had tonight in such raw fashion.

Had he really been swept away, believed the match still in progress, lunged so that he inadvertently caught Colin's unprotected hand? Surely—surely, it couldn't have been deliberate!

And Shana.

Why had she looked so strange, as if sleepwalking in a nightmare? Why had she smeared Colin's blood on her face?

I shivered as I went back to my part of the lodge. The only good thing about the evening, which should have been such fun and sport, was my match with Colin when I had done well, thanks to his way of restoring my confidence. He had called for my best, so that I'd used what I knew creditably, though I'd never had the verve and finesse that Cecile could probably develop, just as I would never dance naked in the mists. I was even unhappy about Colin's taking Cecile home, though it would have been a shame to have ruined her introduction to fencing. I peered out my bedroom window but saw no light on at his cabin.

Well . . . It would take him a while to drive her home and perhaps he had some unfinished chores to see to. I gave Donner and Blitzen a nightcap of milk, had one myself, and wrote a bit on my diary-type letter to Mother before I was driven back to look out my window again.

There was still no light.

I bit my lip, dropped the curtains, and went in the bathroom to get ready for bed. This was ridiculous! I couldn't make a habit of glooming when Colin's cabin was dark, or wondering where he was and with whom and what he was doing!

But it already seemed a habit. Wondering where he was, whom he was with, what he was doing. Oh, damn it! The man might have killed my sister. I couldn't love him, must not.

I scrubbed my face ferociously, rinsing it with water so cold it stung, and was toweling briskly when the dogs set up a chorus. Grasping a robe, I hurried through the hall, switching on the lights in the main room while Donner and Blitzen frisked and barked wildly at the door.

Reassured by their behavior, heart thudding in fear-hope, I called shakily, "Who—who's there?"

"I came back for my stew," Colin answered. "You gave me about a quart of it, remember?"

Not very romantic, that. Still, it was a justifiable reason for knocking on a woman's door at eleven. And I was glad, in spite of stern self-admonition, to know that precociously sexy little Cecile was safely home and Colin was by himself.

I slipped the bolt and turned the knob, stepping back as he came in to be greeted riotously by the dogs. They liked me and didn't whine or lament at night, but the way they leaped on Colin, lavishing licks and ecstacy on him, showed where their first affections lay.

Still, they were reliable watchdogs in alerting me to Colin's presence. Him, they'd greet with joy; Britt, they'd growl at. But either way, I'd be warned. They wouldn't attack Colin for me, that I knew, but somehow I couldn't believe he'd hurt me, though I had to accept the fact that he might have done away with Anne out of jealousy. His emotions would be strong.

And mine were getting that way. I braked them hard and said in a matter-of-fact voice, leading the way to the kitchen, "That was quite an evening. Does Britt always fence that way?"

"I don't know, we haven't had a match in years."

"Really?" I asked, astonished. "With both of you so keen on it, and the isolation here, it would seem a natural kind of pastime."

"There's a first—and often last—time for everything." Colin's tone was dry. "Britt never called me a bastard before, either."

"It was a dirty thing to do."

"But true in the technical sense."

"What galls Britt is probably that he knows you really belong more in Smoke Valley than he does, that you understand cattle and can look after the herds, whereas from what I can see he'd be more at home as English landed gentry, living on an estate in the East with biology for a hobby."

Colin shrugged. "I don't know. We've always rubbed along well enough. He never interferes with my decisions. I see him precious little."

*But how often do you see his wife?*

I turned my head so that Colin couldn't read the unspoken question, busying myself with making sure the snap-type lid was firmly on the stew container.

"Jan."

I looked up, stricken to the depths by his voice, the way he spoke my name. And I knew my face was naked—surely he would read it, take me in his arms. My mind struggled frantically with my body, trying to resume control, but if he had touched me then, I would have melted, I couldn't have helped it.

He kept his distance, though a muscle contracted in his lean jaw. "Jan," he repeated, "would you go riding with me tomorrow? I'd like to show you the trumpeter swans, and it can't be long before the snow falls. A nice long autumn ramble would show you a lot of Smoke Valley."

"That sounds lovely." I swallowed, trying to make my voice less husky. "But I've only been on a horse a couple of times. You'd have to get me a really tame one."

"No problem."

His fingers brushed mine as I handed him the food. Sweet fire shot through me from that slight contact. It took an effort of will not to close my eyes, to go outwardly as limp as I felt.

"Shall I bring lunch?" I asked, forcing a brisk manner.

"No, lunch will be on me, if you like fish," he said.

"Love it!" I stopped in dismay. "But Cecile will be expecting her geometry lesson."

"Phone in the morning. She can have a double dose later. Besides, that's strictly a labor of love, isn't it? Not part of your job."

"I'm glad to do it."

"And she's lucky that you do." His words took on an edge. "God knows, she needs to be around a normal woman!"

"Paula seems kind and healthy."

"She is. And she adores Cecy. But she can scarcely serve as a model for a child like that—Cecy's a devil-child, if you hadn't noticed! Worships you one minute, cuts out your heart the next."

"She's in love with you and you won't take her seriously."

"How can I? She's a baby! Until a year ago, she was like a young brother, fun, quick to learn, ready for anything." He gave a mock shudder that conveyed real distress. "I hope to hell this present stage passes pretty damn quick. She really wants a father, of course, and I can play that to her, but the dumb kid persists in confusing that need with torrid romance." He spread his hands appealingly. "I know with Cecy that one can't be too obvious, she bucks right away. But do what you can, won't you?"

"I don't expect to have much influence with her."

"You'd be surprised. She's already quoting you."

"Really?" I asked, astounded.

"Really. Of course she prefaces such remarks with how prim, proper, and mid-victorian you are, but the admiration and wistfulness show through. Hang in there, Jan. You may give the kid a chance."

"Her mother—"

Colin's mouth thinned. He looked, for a moment, really dangerous, more angry than when he had challenged Britt. "Shana is an odd one. She may not hate Cecile, she may love her in a painful way, but she does see her more and more as a rival, so things are getting stickier than usual around the happy homestead. I suppose it could be worse. Instead of loathing Cecy, Britt could try to seduce her."

A dreadful notion. But one that Cecile—given her low self-esteem and desire to impress Colin with her allure—might just have cooperated with. So, though the enmity between the girl and Britt was hate-engendering, at least it was better than the alternative Colin had suggested.

I was surprised at him imagining such a situation, but after all, he had been relentlessly exposed to the girl's seductiveness and knew more about a man's reaction than I ever could.

Cecile's troubles made me reluctant to cancel our meeting, but I told myself that was absurd, I couldn't allow an easily arranged voluntary session like that to become a manacle, a time-binding mechanism. I'd make up for it by inviting her to lunch the next day and doubling the lesson time.

"All right," I said. "I'll call Cecile in the morning. What time shall we leave?"

"Oh, I'll have to do a few things first. Can you be ready about ten? That won't rush us and we'll be back well before dark."

"Fine," I nodded.

He didn't touch me. "Come lock the door securely," he said, half-teasing, half-earnest.

So I went with him through the hall, and after we said good night, I shot the bolt fast.

"What are you going to be doing?" Cecile demanded when I telephoned next morning to postpone our lesson.

"I'm going riding with Colin. He wants to show me the trumpeter swans."

"Can I come?"

"You'd have to ask him," I said. "He didn't mention it."

"And neither did you," she accused.

"Really, Cecile, you've been all over the place. It never occurred to me that you'd want to visit the swans."

"Well, I do!"

"Then talk to Colin. It's his excursion."

"He'll say no," she said spitefully. "That's all he ever says to me anymore." Her voice rose shrilly. " 'No, no, no! You're too young, Cecy. Be careful, Cecy, don't do that, Cecy!' That's all he ever says to me now!"

"Maybe it's because of what you say to him," I suggested.

"What do you know about what I say to him?" she flashed, and I could picture her: vibrant, defiant, hurt, proud, a child yet blossoming into woman.

I spoke in what I prayed was a calming tone. "I know you—you like him a lot, Cecile. And he cares for you, very deeply. But you scare him."

"I scare him?" she echoed incredulously.

"You certainly do!" I would rather have tackled this, if at all, in person, where I could watch her, gear my words to her response, but the moment had come on us now. I felt I had to at least have a stab at explaining. "Look, Cecile, Colin feels protective about you, like a father or older brother; after all, he is a step-uncle. But you're very beautiful, your body is a lot older than you are right now, and he's a man, he can't keep from responding to you on that level, though all his emotions and thoughts tell him it's wrong, that he must keep his hands off you."

"I wish he wouldn't."

"That would be a dandy mess!" I snapped, in spite of myself. "Can't you understand? That kind of thing is absolutely impossible with you as young as you are."

"Oh, is it?" she mocked.

I took a deep breath and made the only realistic threat I could think of that might influence her at all. "If you ever got what you think you want, he would have to leave Smoke Valley."

"No, he wouldn't. If he loved me—"

"You little idiot, can't you get it through your head that he can't let himself treat you as a woman? That if he did, he'd hate himself, be so ashamed and miserable and afraid of it happening again that he'd have to go away?"

"You're just jealous! You—you want to ruin things for me."

There was some truth in that, but it didn't change the operable facts of life. "Cecile, please listen! There's what—fourteen years between you and Colin?"

"Yes," she acknowledged sulkily.

"That's an unbridgable gap at present, but in six years, maybe even four, it wouldn't be unthinkable. You'd be old enough for him to love you without guilt. Maybe it'll happen, if you don't wreck things now."

She laughed with a funny strangling mixture of heartbreak and derision. "Oh, Jan, you're the naïve young one! You think Colin can be stopped by guilt?"

"What do you mean?" I almost whispered, my heart going cold and still, as if a dead hand had closed on it.

"He's my mother's lover. Didn't you know that?"

It was not a surprise, but confirmation shook me terribly. "You shouldn't say that, even if it's true. Anyway, you're guessing."

"Don't you wish I were!" she taunted. "But I saw them. Saw them at his place, saw them where he's taking you today." And her voice thinned with envy and pain, which reverberated inside me at the thought.

"However that may be," I said, when at last I could speak, "your mother is a mature woman; the guilt would be a lot different. And I wish, Cecile, that you wouldn't tell me things that are—that are none of my business!"

"Things that hurt, you mean."

I gave up on that tack. Maybe she'd at least think over what I'd said about Colin, take some comfort in the bait of a future when she'd be eligible. "Why don't you come over tomorrow in time for lunch?" I invited. "Then we could have an extra long session, maybe take a walk to some place you know."

"Why go with me when Colin will take you?" she said frostily. I could see her nose tilting high in the air, the shake she would give her imperious golden mane. "Thanks very much, but I've got other plans tomorrow. Maybe I'll call you next week."

"It would be better if you didn't skip the geometry too long."

"I'm not sure I care to learn the angles you can teach me," she said, in that preposterous, laughable, but irritating fashion. She softened a little. "However, I'll see you before long, I guess, because the lodge is the best place to fence, and Colin has promised to teach me, if I pay attention. He promised last night."

Poor Colin! Wary as I had to be of him, I could pity his dilemma, wanting to companion this child who needed it so badly, yet terrified of her insistent budding sexuality.

"That's splendid," I said. "And of course, I'll be glad to show you what I can, but it won't take you long to get better than I'll ever be."

"You mean that, truly?" she asked in a reluctantly gratified tone.

"Truly. Sad but true," I laughed, trying to establish friendliness again. In spite of everything, I *did* like the girl, was fascinated by her, did want to help if I possibly could. "Your body and mind are a lot more coordinated than mine, and you interpret an opponent's clues with amazing speed. Oh yes, Cecile, in time you can make a formidable fencer."

"Then I will," she said reflectively. "Because anyhow, Colin's not worried about teaching me that. I suppose he figures that with you around, he can defend himself."

"Wheesh!" I gasped inelegantly. "You do have a single-track mind."

"That's why I'm well-coordinated," she jabbed, with lightning speed. "You don't have a single-track mind, do you, Jan? You wonder about us all, but don't know what to think."

"Who would?" I demanded. "It's a bewildering household."

"You don't know the half of it," she said drily. "Good-bye, then. I'll let you know when I'm ready to take lessons."

"And I'll let you know if it's convenient for me," I replied, carefully maintaining an equable tone.

Surprised bell-like laughter rang out. "You're bewildering, too, in your nice, polite way," she giggled. "All right—I'll call you and request an audience, your highness, please. And I may see you at fencing anyway."

"Fine. Good-bye."

"Enjoy your ride," she gave back, in a tone I couldn't assess. I heard the phone click.

Slowly hanging up, I absently patted Donner and Blitzen.

*Careful,* I warned myself. *Be careful!* There was a chance that Cecile was mistaken or lying about her mother and Colin, but I didn't think so. I had seen Shana in the cabin, remembered that she'd been there the day she was supposed to collect me in Billings.

Whatever was between her and her husband, it wasn't love, and I couldn't imagine she'd have many scruples about taking a lover after the cosmopolitan way she had been brought up and had apparently lived prior to her marriage.

Then, if this relationship existed, how had my sister fitted into it? Had Shana been jealous? Had Anne known the truth? My mind spun wild fantasies, perhapses.

Maybe Anne had found out and, stricken, run off with Nordstrom in retaliation. It made better sense than any other explanation I'd hit on yet. And then?

My head whirled and I pressed my face in my hands, trying to steady myself, fight the overwhelming grief and loss that came when I had to remember that Anne was dead.

If Anne *had* gone with Nordstrom after a. lover's quarrel with Colin, Colin could have followed and killed one or both. Or he might be completely innocent.

How to know? How to find out?

It was swiftly becoming as important to me to know about Colin as it was to learn what had happened to Anne. Of course, the two enigmas probably interlocked. When I knew the answer to one riddle, the other should be solved.

I poured myself a shot of Scotch, though I never drank in the morning. By the time the dogs set up a welcoming clamor, I was *almost* ready to face Colin without, I hoped, betraying my fears and suspicions—and hopes.

# 14

Colin was hitching two horses to the post by the porch, a pinto with dark cherry patches and a mask-like blaze across the face, and the larger horse he must have been riding, a chestnut burnished to bright flame. He quelled Donner and Blitzen who bounded up, heedless of the nervous horses, but then the young dogs spotted their parents, who had sensibly kept some distance from the hitching post, and gamboled over to salute them, frisking and making playful woofs of welcome.

"Ready?" Colin greeted. His eyes lit up as they ran over me, though there was nothing glamorous about my Levi's and heavy plaid jacket. "I brought Neeka for you. She's gentle, but a fancy stepper and no jughead."

"She's beautiful," I murmured, stroking her muzzle, daring gradually to pat her neck. "Hello, Neeka girl! Are we going to see the swans?"

Colin produced an apple. "Give her this and she'll be enamored of you for the day." He pulled another apple out of his saddlebag and proffered it to the splendid chestnut, who crunched away while I gingerly held Neeka's treat toward her.

All horses, I'm sure, have yellow teeth, big ones. And though I know perfectly well that horses eat grass and oats, not people, those teeth make me jumpy when they're close to my hand. Still, she was an understanding beast and consumed the apple neatly, leaving my fingers intact.

"All aboard," said Colin, who had been watching me with a broad grin.

He untied Neeka's reins, came around, and gave me a hand up, though I did know which foot to put in the stirrup. Even through my thick jacket and his gloves, a flash of electrical awareness pierced through me at his touch. I wondered if he felt it, too, if he had given me the unnecessary help in order to feel it.

"Neeka neck-reins," he explained, handing me the reins. "And she's got a tender mouth."

"I'll be easy," I promised, patting her shoulder where the heavy winter coat was already showing.

Colin swung up in one smooth motion, gathered his reins, and turned his horse, making a little clucking sound. "Let's go, Charlie," he said.

"Charlie!" I said indignantly. "You call that gorgeous animal Charlie?"

"Why not?" laughed Colin, turning his head toward me. "His whole name is Bonnie Prince Charlie, but that's a mouthful. He knows his lineage. Like true royalty, he needn't stand on ceremonies and salutations because he *is* the best." He slapped his horse's gleaming flank. "Huh, Charlie? We'll have to teach this flatland foreign gal some things."

The four black dogs ran ahead, beside, and sometimes behind us, sniffing joyously, barking when they scented anything warranting the attention of the others. It reminded me of those medieval tapestries in which lovers ride out hunting with their dogs and falcons, except we had no falcons and we were hunting swans to look at, not deer to kill.

A peaceable hunt, a happy one.

Foreboding quickly chilled that lighthearted fancy. I must not forget, ever, that this man had loved my sister, might have killed her, or that he was Shana's lover. He was dangerous.

*All right,* some part of me returned, *I'll remember. But meanwhile, I'm going to enjoy the day, and being with him, and what we see. And whatever happens later, this will be a good time and a happy one.*

Is that defying fate, to try to separate a period or experience from what has been and what will be?

Maybe so. I'm sure it's defying common sense, which is too often a synonym for playing safe, for sticking to the known, passing up a potential but uncertain feast for the immediate gratification of a good Salisbury steak, or more appropriately to my situation, refusing to eat mushrooms on the chance of getting a poisonous toadstool.

It was a magic day—clear, sunny, just crisply chill enough to bring blood tingling to the face. We turned off the main road on a rough way marked by ruts, which looked like a four-wheel drive had used it, as well as horses whose tracks showed in the outer patches of dried mud.

"We'll go by Samson's pasture," Colin said. "We had to move him over here because when he was in the holding pasture not far from the house, he was always jumping the fence and eating Shana's flowers. For the sake of peace, I'm hoping his offspring are more bovine than he in temperament."

I wondered if Cecile had asked Colin if she could go with us, but decided to leave it alone. It seemed wise to me to keep out of the emotional tangle involving Colin, Shana, and Cecile. Besides, Cecile might ask if I had asked, and I wanted to be able to tell her no.

The track came out to parallel a barbed wire fence stringing off far out of sight. Colin stopped Charlie and pointed. Far away, I saw a shaggy, oblong-looking creature, rather like a hair-covered box with a head.

"There's our boy," said Colin. "When we're closer, you'll get a better look. His cows and calves are further back in the woods. See 'em?"

It took a few minutes, but I did finally make out the scattered little herd, merged with the trunks and shadows of the trees. "Do you think the cross is going to do what you want?" I asked.

"The hybrids seem more self-reliant and aggressive than their mothers," Colin evaluated. "They can forage in snow, using their hoofs to knock off the snow, just like Papa. But how their offspring, if any, will function, is the real question. Otherwise our shaggy friend Samson here will just have been a pretty wild and interesting experiment."

"Like Britt's?" I couldn't help asking.

Colin's brows rushed together. "*Not* like Britt's!" he said violently. "Nothing gets hurt in this little riff with the yaks except an occasional rosebush or flower bed."

This was a confirmation—implied, at least—of what I had feared. "I thought Britt just observed hibernating creatures," I ventured. "The ones I saw looked all right except they were in cages."

"That would be enough in itself," Colin said grimly. "Animals don't belong in cages."

"You mean—Britt really experiments? With injections and so on?"

"Ask him," advised Colin. "I have nothing whatsoever to do with his little games, except I told him if he ever tried jailing any pikas, I'd tear up all his damned cages."

"He thinks there'd be some dramatic advantages to people if the key to hibernation were understood," I persisted.

"Yes, that's what he would tell you."

"What do you mean?"

"Damn it to hell!" Colin exploded. "I can remember when Britt used to vacation here—that's right, he was educated in England and only spent holidays here till he was eighteen—I remember what he called sport! Hunting coyotes and eagles in a monoplane, buzzing coyotes, literally running them to death."

"Could—could you stop him?"

"Yes," said Colin, briefly. He half-turned in the saddle. "Jan, listen. Don't get mixed up with us here. It's not safe. Britt hates me, but he needs me to run the place. I hate him, but I love Smoke Valley."

"And where does Shana fit?"

"She doesn't." Colin glanced away. "She doesn't fit at all."

Into what? His dreams, his life, what he'd have chosen if he could have? But if he cared for her, could he have loved Anne, too, or had he wanted to love someone who was at least theoretically available?

Pain and jealousy, both for my sister and myself, gnawed at me in a deeply visceral fashion. I tried to deny it, shove it away, by concentrating on the yak as we came nearer.

His coarse gray hair fell like a long-stranded cotton dust mop from a center part along the backbone, curtaining his body all the way to his neat small hooves. Bright intelligent eyes gleamed warily from more hair, and his wicked horns bowed like a rather pot-bellied lyre atop his head.

*Come closer,* his stance said, *and I'll show you whose domain this is!*

But we stayed outside the fence, and when I looked back a few minutes later, Samson had gone back to grazing in his sentinel-liege position.

"We'd see more animals if the dogs weren't questing around," Colin said. "Of course, early morning and late afternoon are the best times to see them anyhow."

But we saw banks of late wildflowers and rocks painted with lichens that ranged from bright red to black and green, caught glimpses of pikas hurling themselves from one miniature precipice to another, or licking their faces like small cats, and once Colin pointed out the golden flash of a weasel pursuing a pika.

"He probably won't catch the pika," Colin said comfortingly at my gasp of distress. "I've watched pikas help each other when a weasel gets into their mazes after trying to catch one. When he's exhausted, another pika will jump out and confuse the weasel, and then another will cut in, and pretty soon the weasel gets tired and dis-

136

gusted, and goes hunting for easier food. It's the same trick small birds often use on a hawk. When he's after one, they eddy around, mixing him up till he can't catch anything because he can't decide on a single target."

"So much for the laws of self-preservation," I said, feeling cheered in spite of the disturbing revelations about Britt and my anxieties about this tall man leading the way on his gleaming chestnut.

"Beyond the simple rule of self-preservation, there seems to be in many cases an overriding urge for species preservation and cooperation," Colin said. "Mankind is by no means the only species to practice 'Women and children first.' Most creatures instinctively know that in their females and young lie the ongoing existence of their group, and this enhanced survival seems coded into behavior. Males are dispensable once they have reproduced."

"It's refreshing to hear a male admit that!"

Colin grinned. "Why not, honey, we can sure have a lot of fun first! And leave you gals to fetch up the children."

"Had to be a catch to it," I said with mock bitterness, making a face at him.

Colin's gaze focused on a slope and, following it. I held my breath, reining up. A mass of elk had appeared on the hilltop, for all the world like those suddenly erupting ranks of Sioux warriors in an old Western.

"How—how many can there be?" I marveled.

"Maybe a hundred. I've seen several hundred at a time now and then."

"Fantastic!"

Even at this distance, I could see the variation in antlers, some only single spikes, others heavily beamed and tined. Many of the herd had no antlers at all, and some were clearly juveniles.

A bugling sound cut through the air and the herd vanished as suddenly as they had appeared.

"That was a bull elk," Colin explained. "This is the

time when they start rounding up their harems. They'll move back to their summering grounds in May, and after that the cows will hunt deep cover to bear their calves, while males move on to higher ground for the summer. But in the fall, groups congregate again."

"Just like men," I jabbed. "Running off while the females have babies and get them trained."

"It does seem a good system," Colin agreed blandly. "Wonder when we'll advance to it?"

He was as difficult to fence with words as with foils. I spent a few minutes trying to think of a blasting comeback, gave it up, and instead pressed for information.

"Shana was educated in England, too, wasn't she? And she must have hunted. That picture in the hall—"

"Yes, that painting was roughed the day after she'd been blooded." Colin's voice was scathing, deeply angry. "Her father was proud that she'd finally been initiated into the royal sport, running a fox into a hole or culvert, digging it out, and letting the hounds tear it up. Very sporting." He mimicked Britt's intonation: " 'But how else, old man, are you to control foxes? It's better than trapping. Anyhow, foxes love it, they enjoy pitting their wits against the pack.' "

"You hunt?"

"Sometimes. But not with hounds, and only quarry that has more chance to get away than I have to kill it." He shrugged. "I don't defend it, Jan. I'm a predator, but I have my rules."

I returned to Shana. "In that portrait, Shana looks dazed. Petrified."

"She was. They had washed the blood off her face, of course. What she needed was a psychiatrist to explain to her the madness of society and her nutty family, but instead she got her portrait done with that fox's brush in her hand."

"When you say 'blooded,' what do you mean exactly?"

"The custom may be dying out now, but Shana's father, perhaps because of his long sojourn in Jamaica, was of the old school. He rubbed his daughter's face with the blood of the fox."

I flinched so hard Neeka sidestepped, forcing me back to reality, the sun dappling a track that led now beneath aspens glittering gold among spruce and fir.

"How terrible!" I breathed.

"It snapped something in her." Colin sighed heavily and again swift jealousy knifed through me. "I wonder what she'd be like if she'd never been made to hunt like that. But," he added fatalistically, "I suppose she was unstable to begin with. No single instance sends someone off balance unless the ground's shaky."

"But isn't everyone on shaky ground?" I demanded. I certainly was! Being irresistibly drawn to this man whose secrets might be a lot more spooky than Britt's or Shana's.

"Some ground is shakier," Colin said. "And some people have fine balance wherever they stand." His eyes touched me, questioned me.

I had no answer for them, no answer for him till I knew his truth, and so I fought down the welling excitement his presence caused and scanned the forests.

We had been climbing gradually. Now we emerged from thick timber and rode into meadowland, a long valley that grew marshy as we went further into it. Sedges grew high about sloughs and lakes, and there we saw the swans.

Huge birds they seemed, some treading shallows, churning up plants which they then immersed themselves to gather, others floating on the water, and even more of them moving on the spongy land with strong legs like movable roots.

"They're so white except for those yellow stains on their heads and necks," I said. "And look at all the young ones!"

"Yes, the cygnets are mostly able to fly by now. Those stains are from the iron in the water. And see those red streaks on the lower beak? That's called a grin line."

"Are they hunted?"

"They're protected under federal law, but they were almost extinct in the thirties—only sixty-six reported then in the whole U.S., though once they ranged from Alaska to Iowa and Missouri, and wintered from the Carolinas to the Pacific. We almost did them in. Hudson's Bay Company sold thousands of swanskins to the London market for ornaments, powder puffs, and down. Even Audubon preferred trumpeter quills for drawing, saying they were much harder and more elastic than the best steel pen."

"It's good to have friends," I whistled.

"Yeah, they just love you to death," Colin agreed wryly. "Anyway, a refuge was established, and breeding colonies were started in Oregon, Nevada, and Wyoming, as well as the original refuge in Montana. Trumpeters are far from numerous, but they're coming back."

We had stopped some distance from the marshy lakes, but the birds must have become frightened, perhaps of the dogs, for suddenly those wading about, or churning up vegetation, fairly bombed through the water for perhaps a hundred feet, then lifted off the surface like miraculous craft, retracting their feet under their tails, their great wings, some surely seven and eight feet in span, thrusting strongly into the air.

Their resonant bugling—a sound of harsh trumpets—floated down to us. They flashed in the sun, sparkling, incredibly beautiful. Exactly twelve of them, so that I caught my breath and remembered the old fairy tale of the twelve princes whose wicked stepmother changed them into swans. If these only had golden crowns . . .

"Let's go so they can come back," Colin said. He reined Charlie toward the opposite rim of forest climbing into the mountains.

"Do the swans migrate?" I asked.

"No, the underground heat that causes the geysers warms this water, too."

"How much do they weigh? They look immense!"

"The adults are twenty to thirty pounds. And now I

hope to introduce you to the best trout lunch you've ever had!"

I didn't tell him I hadn't had many, and those had been so lamentable that I was nervous about this one. I kept looking backward to the high points of light which were the swans, sighing as they circled and gracefully floated down, out of sight among the sedges.

We were in more trees, fir and spruce, riding along a stream that soon fed into a wide deep blue lake, with several small islands jutting here and there in its expanse. On the distant side marched a row of jagged mountains, backed by higher peaks, and over it all hung a sunny haze that made the blue softer, the mountains dreamy.

Colin got down and helped me out of the saddle before he watered the horses, hitched them in a grassy spot, and loosened their girths.

"Now," he said, "will you have a fishing lesson or would you like to wander a bit?"

"Wander, please," I said cravenly, for the truth was that I would eat a fish, but didn't like to see it caught.

So while Colin produced a telescoping rod from a case on his saddle, I called the dogs and ranged along the lake for perhaps a half-mile till a puff of floating vapor I had come to associate with geysers and fumaroles signaled from the trees.

Taking mental note of my location, I moved into the woods and soon located the vapor flats. Little streams trickled over brightly colored rocks, and at one pool I saw hummingbirds. Approaching cautiously, I also noticed that fumes from the heated pool must have been toxic to some degree, for many insects, and even one bird, lay dead in its waters or on its margin.

So there we were again, the constant natural cycle of life and death. I gave the dogs, who were pushing at my hands, absent-minded pats and soothing words as I turned back toward the lake.

Much as I dreaded what I might find out, soon, very soon, I had to start pressing to learn about Anne. But not today. Just for today, I'd experience Colin. And if later, he proved to be a murderer or just a man who romanced all the female lodge staff, at least there'd be this day to remember, this bright day of swans.

# 15

I could smell a tantalizing aroma before I stepped out of the woods. The smell--and my hunger—grew as I came nearer the fire built between two rocks on which Colin had placed a skillet.

Two fish sizzled away in the pan. "Cuthroat trout," said Colin, grinning. "Great fighters. These are small. I've taken eight-pounders here, but I figured we'd take what came first today, since it's getting late."

He had the rest of our lunch neatly arranged on a rock slab—a Thermos of coffee, lemon to squeeze on the trout, hunks of brown bread, and two Golden Delicious apples.

When the fish were done, he put the skillet on the rock, and we helped ourselves, using bread for plates to hold the tender succulent fish.

The ride and fresh air had made me ravenous. I consumed all of the smallest fish, my bread, apple, and two cups of coffee. Then, replete, I felt drowsy.

Colin read my mind. "Here," he said, peeling off his jacket. "Put this under your head and have a nap."

I hadn't the strength, moral or physical, to argue. Lying back on his jacket, I felt pleasantly beguiled by the aroma of tobacco, woodsmoke, and general outdoorsiness. The sun warmed me, my contented stomach purred, and I fell into a kind of light velvety slumber, my mind blank though my senses were partially aware, senses that suddenly jarred me awake.

I opened my eyes and looked at Colin, who stood a few feet away. It must have been the intensity of those gray eyes, now turning me helpless, meltingly weak, that had roused me.

"Goodness, I hope I didn't snore," I said, grasping for lightness, starting to sit up.

But he lay down by me and carried me back with him.

"You—you said you wouldn't do that—till I asked you!" I cried indignantly when his mouth finally left mine, when my mind cleared enough to remember that I was outraged.

"Your eyes asked me," he said.

"What an excuse!" Only the thought of Anne gave me strength to move out of reach, keep my tone icy. "It would seem Britt was right after all. Of course I suppose since I'm the only staff around right now, you have to go to a little more trouble. Take me riding, give me lunch—"

"Do you believe that?"

I could meet his gray eyes only for a moment, but I jumped up, thrust his jacket back at him, and began collecting the food things.

"I don't understand you," Colin said slowly. It sounded as if it were costing him something to pursue the matter at all. "I'm not trying to seduce you, not all at once, anyway. Why are you so damned edgy?"

"I guess I've known too many girls who weren't edgy—till it was too late."

He gave up with a shrug. "Fair enough." He packed the skillet and Thermos, tightened the horses' girths, and then, infuriatingly, gave me a cool grin. "Okay, honey. I won't read your pretty eyes anymore. You want another kiss and you *will* ask, for sure."

"I'll never—"

"Oh, come on, mount up!" he said good-naturedly,

making me feel really childish, a Victorian prude. "Kisses aren't a matter of life and death, but if you're still young enough to think they are, that settles it." He gave me a boost and handed me the reins.

Neeka exploded.

I shot off, clutching for the saddlehorn, the reins, anything to grasp, but I was on the ground, knocked breathless, before I knew what had happened. Knocked senseless, too, for seconds, because when I opened my eyes, Colin had the pinto mare under control, holding her head down.

"You go crazy?" he asked her, somehow mingling anger and reassurance in his tone. He looked at me. "Jan? You all right?"

"I—I think so."

Gingerly stretching, I sat up and discovered nothing was broken, though I imagined later I'd be sore around my back and shoulders where I'd taken the impact of the fall. Colin gave me a hand up but kept a tight grip on Neeka.

"I can't understand it," he said, knitting his brows. "She's never done such a thing, not even when she was being broken. It was as if—"

He broke off, loosened the girth, and ran his fingers beneath the back flap of the saddle. "Well, I'll be damned!" he said, staring at what he held between his thumb and forefinger.

A small pine cone. Not big enough to cause trouble till my weight mashed it down, sending its sharp edges into Neeka's back. "So that was it," he said.

I just stared at him. Was he going to say he hadn't done it? If he hadn't, who had? His gray eyes read my thoughts.

"You think I set that up?" He snapped the cone away with a snap of his wrist. "Now why on earth would I?"

"I—I don't know." My breath was still short, and my shoulders ached where I'd hit hardest. "But it didn't get there by force of gravity or something."

"No, someone put it there," he agreed. "Must have

been while I was fishing and you were on your walk." He pondered, scowled, saying without conviction, "Maybe it was somebody's idea of a joke."

"You know you don't believe that."

"No, I don't." His voice was grave. "Jan, who'd want to hurt you? Maybe even kill you, because it could have happened if you'd snapped your neck or hit a rock."

"I don't know. I don't think anyone does."

But a vision of Cecile's face rose before me: jealous, vindictive, as it must have been when I had told her she must ask Colin if she could go with us today. He, in his unsettling way of guessing my thoughts, detected that flash.

"Whom did you think of just now?"

I didn't want to say. After all, I wasn't hurt, and though Cecile might be jealous, I knew she was warming to me, and her starved nature needed that. If I accused her—well, any hope of being her friend would be wrecked.

"Spit it out," ordered Colin, hands on his hips. He towered over me till I felt intimidated, and that made me angry.

"It was nothing, I tell you! Forget it."

"Don't you realize, little idiot, that you could be dead?" Colin's breath rasped out and I retreated from his range. "Why should you want to protect anyone at Smoke Valley? I haven't seen that they've been *that* good to you."

"I'm not going to throw around wild accusations," I retorted. "*You* happen to be the most likely person, don't you know that? And all this third degree after your plot failed could simply be cover-up."

He looked absolutely astounded. I drove the point home. "After all, you've loosened the horses' girths, handled them. The presence of anybody else is strictly conjecture. If I *had* to name a suspect right now, it would be you!"

He looked baffled beyond measure. I hardened my heart, keeping an aggressive eye on him. What I'd said

146

was true, and his shocked, stunned manner could be masterful acting to take me in.

"Why?" he asked. "Why on earth, Jan, would I hurt you?"

*Maybe you've learned I'm Anne's sister. Maybe you're afraid of being found out if you killed her. Or maybe you're a psychopath who likes his women with broken necks, how do I know?*

Out of the welter of fear, anger, love, and suspicion, I forged my words clear and hard. "I don't know! Why would you?"

His mouth clamped tight. "I wouldn't. I didn't. But I suppose you're right from your standpoint." His eyes darkened. "I've got a theory or two, but if you've no reason to reinforce them, I'll simply poke around on my own hook. And meanwhile, be careful!"

He helped me mount again, and though Neeka fidgeted a bit, I stroked and calmed her. I wasn't even very nervous, since that jagged pine cone explained her previous behavior. We rode home by a loop verging on the mountains, the four black dogs trailing like shadows, but though now and then Colin would point out a squirrel or bird or lichen, mostly we were silent.

I couldn't know what was in his mind, but what was in mine was a kind of deadly chant. *Someone wants to hurt you, kill you. Someone wants to at least frighten you.*

Cecile, from jealousy? Shana? Britt, from some perverse motivation? Colin? He, alas, was the prime target, just from practical considerations. Hard to believe he'd make love to me one moment and try murder the next, but if he had killed Anne, the pattern would be the same.

There was a faint chance that some passerby had done it for a joke, but what passerby? There weren't any near neighbors, the lodge had no guests, and certainly no Smoke Valley cowboy would try such a thing unless he was warped.

No, however I strained it, likelihood sifted down to Cecile, who had known where we were going, and to

Colin. I hated to suspect either, but there it was.

It was twilight when Colin left me at the lodge with Donner and Blitzen, who were amiable enough about parting with their parents and following me inside. Perhaps they had reached the age when Mom and Dad were glad to see them independent.

Colin helped me down from Neeka, but he didn't let his hands linger. "Good night, Jan. I'm sorry you took that fall."

So was I, and not only because of my sore back and shoulders. "Good night, Colin. It was—a beautiful ride."

"Anyway?" He grinned suddenly, and pressed my hand. "Listen, I didn't pull that trick, but I'll find out who did. Meanwhile, if you get any ideas or feel nervous, call me. I do have a phone in my log cabin."

"Thanks," I said, feeling better, even if I still did have to suspect him.

I locked the doors, fed the dogs and myself, had a hot shower to ease my bruised body, and went to bed early.

The next morning I tackled a double quota of rooms upstairs, finished up by noon, and was devouring a massive sandwich which I had carried out to the verandah, when a jeep churned up, Shana at the wheel.

"Have you seen Cecile?" she demanded, almost before she swung out of the vehicle, reed-slender in pale green suede riding clothes, her golden hair massed back with a green ribbon.

I swallowed what I had in my mouth. "No. I thought she might come for geometry today, though she'd said something about not having lessons for a little while."

"The little devil!" Shana grated, staring about as if at her wit's end. "I can't find her. Can't find her anyplace!"

My heart skidded. If Cecile had put that cone under my saddle, she might have waited to see what happened—and when she saw the trick was discovered, she might have been afraid to come home, afraid to face Colin or me.

"When did you see her last?" I asked, forcing my voice to sound calm.

Shana pushed away a few strands of loose hair. "Yesterday morning. But she's off rambling so much that I didn't worry about it—she often eats in the kitchen or snacks in her room. So I didn't know she was gone till I looked in her room this morning. Her bed hadn't been slept in. Paula hasn't seen her since yesterday. No one has." She looked at me in a cross between appeal and accusation. "She's fond of you. You really don't know where she is?"

I shook my head. "Have you asked Colin?"

Her eyes changed, dropped from mine. "Yes. He hasn't seen her either." And what else had he said, I wondered? "Her horse is gone. That's all we know."

So she could be in Misty Basin, or in the vale of wild flowers, or hiding beyond the lake, or—" Do you suppose she might have gone to visit Tam Cannon?" I asked.

Shana's head snapped back. "Of course, that must be it!" she cried. "She could go up to the north cabin, worry me to death, stay there all winter, the little wretch! Tam wouldn't tell if she lied enough—he hates me anyway!" She clenched her fists till the knuckles stood out in white ridges, then swung toward the jeep. "I'm going right up there and show them I won't stand for this!"

"Now, Shana, it's just a possibility," I protested. "Besides, there may have been some reason why she didn't get home last night. She might have had an accident." Watching Shana narrowly, I added in a casual way, "Why, I got thrown yesterday, and Colin says Neeka's tame as a kitten. So—"

"Don't blither!" snapped my employer. Her face instantly showed contrition. "I'm sorry, I truly am, Jan, but I'm overwrought. Cecile and I—we had words yesterday, stormier than usual. I—I've been afraid she might do something really wild. The silly infant is always threatening some bizarre form of suicide. Jumping into a geyser, inhaling poison gases from some fumarole—anything to get me frantic! And she couldn't fall off her horse, she's a brilliant rider. Might have been thrown, of course, or the horse could have plunged down a canyon, but—" She drew a long breath. "Tam hasn't a phone, so I've got to go out. And if she's not there, Tam must help look for her, he knows all her favorite places."

"May I go with you?" I asked. "I'm worried, too."

Shana looked grateful. There was no doubt that she loved her daughter, however twisted and tortured the affection had become.

"Thanks," she said, climbing gracefully into the jeep. "I'd like the company." Her face looked haggard in spite of its beauty. "Especially if Cecile isn't there. Oh, God, why does she act the way she does, why does she keep on and on till—"

Breaking off, she started the engine. We drove past Colin's place, took the Billings road for a little way, then turned sharply west.

"Colin's gone to look in Misty Basin," Shana explained. "Britt's ridden up by the lake. And we've got the men hunting along the high trails. Funny none of us thought about Tam. I guess she's so infatuated with Colin that it didn't occur to anyone that she might have holed up that far away."

There didn't seem anything useful to reply to that. I gripped the edge of the seat as we bounced along the gullied road that snaked through a pass in the mountains, crossed a wide meadow, and then climbed, doing hairpin turns that sometimes let you look back down at three levels where you'd already been.

Dizzying. My stomach knotted in a tight ball and I stopped looking when the sheer drops were on my side. Shana drove with skill and astonishing conservatism—not that she had much choice, on that road.

"You say Neeka threw you yesterday?" she inquired, though earlier her expression hadn't changed when I'd tossed out the information. "Apparently you weren't hurt."

"Just shaken up."

Shana laughed a bit distractedly. "My dear, I don't have to be thrown from a horse to feel that way! But it is surprising. Neeka's the gentlest horse we have who still has spirit, and Colin broke her himself so that she wouldn't pick up bad habits." I thought the smile she cast me was slightly malicious. "Colin, you see wanted one nice easy mount for his lady companions, many of whom had never sat a horse before."

My heart pounded and it was lucky that my tensed position disguised any new tautness. Had Anne ridden Neeka? And here was Shana corroborating that Colin did indeed have an eye for transient girls. I knew that she was deliberately giving me the information, and I refused to answer it.

Should I tell her about the pine cone? I decided not to. If Cecile had planted it, there was no use getting her into more trouble. If Colin had, I didn't want Shana to know, even if the rational thing would have been to tell her what had happened and that he was the logical suspect.

"Neeka is easy to ride," I said. "Something must have startled her."

Which was true enough, as far as it went. Which seemed further than I could trust what anyone here said. What confusion! Cecile stating that Shana and Colin were lovers, Shana saying her daughter was mad for him, all of them saying he had done more than dutifully entertain girls from the lodge. Among whom was almost certainly my sister.

How could I learn more about Anne without revealing that I knew her, or making the possibly guilty person suspicious?

"It must be rather a worry to you," I said at last, coming up with what seemed to me a perfectly normal line of reasoning. "All these young women who work at the lodge. In a way, you must feel responsible for them."

"To a degree, naturally." Shana's voice was without enthusiasm. "However, we have certain rules, and the cook serves as a sort of dorm mother, letting me know if

any girl is consistently out late or disporting herself unduly."

"Does that happen often?"

"Oh, several times a season, usually." Shana gave a lift
of her shoulders. "Sometimes a talk straightens them out.
Now and then they just have to leave."

"That must be a nuisance."

But my sympathy elicited no lurid details about "a girl
last summer who. . . ." In fact, Shana let the conversation
lapse, and I could think of no way to renew it without
sounding overinsistent.

We were in high country now, on a wooded plateau.
Shana spun the jeep through a rocky defile and pulled
up by a cabin nestled into the flank of a hill.

On a bench in front sat Tam, mending what looked
like a bridle. Cecile was at his feet on a log.

# 16

The sun glinted on a needle in the girl's hand, flaming through the blaze of her hair as she jumped up, eyes wide, mouth open. She still held one woolly man's sock, but a clutch of others fell from her lap. Scissors and pincushion showed what she had been doing, though she slipped her hands with the betraying needle and sock behind her as if caught in some crime.

Haughty Cecile, mending an old cowboy's socks!

But my amazed, relieved stare was pulled from the girl by Shana who sat behind the wheel, gripping it tight, breathing in scary little gasps.

"What's wrong?" I said, afraid she was having some kind of attack. She ignored me. Her voice cut the silence like a rasping knife.

"I—I'm trying hard, very hard, Cecile, not to walk over and slap your face off! What do you mean, coming up here, frightening me to death?"

Cecile was as pale as she could ever get beneath her natural and sun-given gold, but she gave her mother a look so contemptuous, so full of hate, that even I shrank from it.

"You don't care where I go," she hurled. "You don't care what happens to me!"

Shana sat for a moment as if transfixed by a spear.

Then she sprang out of the jeep, crossed to her daughter, and swung her palm around with the full force of her body behind it.

Cecile staggered back a few paces, checked herself, and stood motionless. Her eyes blazed, though, and her mouth was distorted. "Do it again," she said in a strange, thin voice. "Do it again—Mother."

Tam was between them. "Go home, Miz Lindsay. Get along. I'll bring Cecy later."

"You old hulk!" Shana hissed. "Egging her on, petting her when she's impossible! What do you know about children?"

"A damn sight more than you, ma'am." Shriveled as he was, Tam somehow managed to rock back on his boot heels and look down a weathered nose at his employer.

"What—what's she been telling you?"

Tam put down the bridle and wiped his hands on his Levi's. "She ain't been tellin' me nothin', leastways not about you," he said calmly. "We been talking about Samson and the colts we look for next spring and—things you don't know about, Miz Lindsay, much less care. You got a great little gal here and you just seem set on ruinin' her! You know that? Do you?"

"Mind your own business, you old fool!" Shana raged.

"I reckon Cecy is my business, ma'am, just like any other young thing growin' up in Smoke Valley."

Shana's lips curled. She glanced from him to her daughter, then suddenly relaxed. "You're fired, Tam. Just forget all your weighty responsibilities and get down to town before the snows come."

"Mother, you can't do that!" cried Cecile.

"Of course I can. I have."

"Tam didn't know we'd had a fight, Mother! I didn't tell him, honest!" Cecile pleadingly caught her mother's arm. "He thought you knew where I was."

"That's immaterial. I won't have an insolent doddering old wreck criticizing me, conniving with an ungrateful little runaway slut—"

"Shut your mouth, Miz Lindsay!" Tam had at first

looked astounded, then crushed, but now he seemed himself again, called back to the old days of guns and showdowns. "Colin is the foreman. I don't take walking papers from anyone else. Now you go home. I'll have Cecy there by suppertime."

Shana looked from one to the other. Cecy had slipped her hand protectively over Tam's, and I thought I saw hurt—furious, humiliated hurt—mingled with the anger on Shana's face.

"You can pick up your time from Colin after you've delivered Cecile," she told Tam.

She flung herself into the jeep and we were away in a crunching, spinning whirl that completely flipped my churning stomach. We were some distance down the road before I could trust myself not to be sick. Shana drove with ferocious intensity, aiming the jeep as if it were an extension of herself with which she could batter down anything in her way.

A deer leaped in front of us. Shana didn't slow down. I screamed. The deer barely whisked by. I began to shake violently.

"Shana!" I called, the wind snatching away my words. "Mrs. Lindsay! You—you're driving too fast!"

She seemed not to hear. But after a few more minutes, she pulled over to the side, put her face in her hands, and wept. Hard, wracking sobs that seemed to shatter without bringing relief.

Appalled as I had been at her behavior at the cabin, I felt sorry for her, but I hadn't the faintest notion of what to do. At last I said, "Shana, I—I'm sorry."

Now tears came. After a while, she sat up, produced a linen handkerchief, and dried her eyes. "Can you understand?" she asked urgently, turning to me. "I love that child more than anyone on this earth, but she drives me to absolute fury! She's hateful and insulting and never says one nice word to me, though she'll trail Colin like a pup and even mend that grubby old cowboy's worn-out socks! It isn't fair, it isn't! And now she'll be worse than ever."

"If you'd change your mind about Tam—"

"I won't!" Her blue eyes slitted. "He's a bad influence, makes her totally unmanageable, and he's going!"

I wondered what Colin would have to say about that, but this was clearly no time to push.

"Girls are pretty difficult at that age anyway," I consoled. "They're confused, having a hard time getting sorted out physically and emotionally, and their mothers are sort of what they have to both measure up to and reject."

Shana gave an impatient wave of her hand. "You know damned well that Cecile's attitude is ten times worse than an average girl's. If I'd talked to my mother the way she talks to me—"

"Cecile's not an average girl," I argued. "Besides, I think she feels pushed out. Britt *is* your husband, and he doesn't seem to like her."

"The understatement of the century," laughed Shana bitterly. "But Cecile's the reason why he is my husband."

I frowned my puzzlement. Shana went on recklessly, as if indulging in long-feared but much-desired release. "I married Britt so that Cecile, who was a baby then, would have a father in name. My parents cut me off after I wouldn't have an abortion, and Britt was crazy for me." An aching smile twitched at the edge of her mouth. "He knew everything, that Cecile's father was black, that I still loved him, but Britt said it didn't matter, he'd take me home to the wild free West, love my child as his own, and we'd be ecstatically happy. All of us. Funny, no?"

"No," I said.

"I should have known better." She stared blindly at the towering peaks, the bright blue sky. Was she remembering Jamaica, the time of her youth, under a hotter sun? "But Darcy couldn't marry me, he had a wife he *loved,* he said. I was just a passing attraction, an exotic treat."

"Did he know about Cecile?"

"Yes. He offered to pay for an abortion, too. Oh, hell, Jan, everyone was generous *that* way! But if all I could have of him was the child, I wanted that . . ."

*And so you have her, and now where are things at?*

"Shocked?" she demanded, face hardening, blue eyes hacking at me as if to chip away any pretense.

"Surprised, I guess. And sorry. It hasn't been easy for any of you."

"And it's not getting better!" She stuffed her handkerchief in her pocket, revved the engine, and we started on, making the rest of the drive in silence.

Her life was a mess of such proportions and complexity that I felt unable to mouth cheering slogans and advice-column wisdom. Still, I longed to say: *Don't fire Tam. It's not fair and will only make Cecile harder to you. Leave her space to grow. In time, maybe, she'll understand. And can't you see that your having Colin, whom she wants, as your lover, makes peace between you and her absolutely impossible on biological grounds alone?*

But I said nothing. Later I always wondered if it might have changed things if I had, but I didn't think she'd listen, and besides, I didn't want to get so involved with any of these people that I'd be trapped by pity if and when I learned that they'd played a part in my sister's death.

Cecile turned up next noon while I was eating a bowl of stew on the veranda. "Can I have a lesson today?" she asked.

"Why not? We can do a little foil practice, too, if you'd like."

I immediately thought: *Supposing she lets her foil "slip"?* But then I reminded myself that they were blunted, and anyway, if I wanted to help this child, I had to risk myself. She was worth that; I had had my mind made up when I saw her darning Tam's raddled socks. Besides, how many girls can dance naked in mists?

"Did you have a nice day with Colin on the lake?" she asked, sinking down on the step, dangling one long leg.

"Gorgeous, except for one little thing."

She lifted her slender golden eyebrows. "What was that?"

Trying with all my might to read her face, I kept my tone light. "Someone thought it would be amusing to put a pine cone under Neeka's saddle. She went up like a thunderbolt the minute I touched the saddle."

Cecile's eyes widened and her mouth dropped open. If she was acting, she was good at it. "Neeka bucked?"

"She did." I grimaced, moving my shoulders which were stiffer today than they had been the day before.

"You're sure about the pine cone?"

"Of course I'm sure! Colin found it."

"He never told *me!*" She looked and sounded annoyed, which annoyed *me,* since I thought she should have exhibited more concern about damage to my skin and bone. "Maybe," she went on, thinking out loud, "he was too upset about Tam to remember."

"He *didn't* fire Tam?"

"You just bet not!" Cecile chuckled wickedly, so that in spite of myself I felt sorry for Shana. "She had given Colin the word before Tam and I jogged down around sunset. But Colin must have given her some words back, because he stopped Tam and told me to go on home alone, that Tam wasn't fired and never would be as long as he was foreman."

"I hope you didn't rub it in," I said, but without much hope.

Cecile's eyes retained their willful glint. "I just told Mother that I'd finished mending all of Tam's socks to last him through the winter. She should have known Colin wouldn't fire him. And she's not about to fire Colin!"

There was not a touch of sympathy in the girl's tone, but admonitions wouldn't put it there. Neither had I been able to detect any significant reaction to my announcement about Neeka's throwing me.

Cecile and I worked on geometry for an hour, and then put on practice jackets. I showed her how to lunge, disengage, beat, and parry, with the discouraging certainty that by spring she'd be running circles around me.

By the end of that hour I was winded, though she was fresh and eager for more. "Tomorrow!" I pleaded.

"All right," she conceded. "And just as soon as I learn a little more, let's get Colin over. Britt, too," she added feistily. "I'm going to get so good I can really pin his ears back, knock his foil right out of his hand!"

"When you can do that, you'll be an expert," I counseled ruefully, remembering my own discomfiture with Britt. "Don't count on it anytime soon."

Her white teeth flashed. "I'll be lucky," she crooned. "The expert stuff can wait. You'll see. I have luck. Got it from my black daddy."

Did she know the truth about that daddy, that he had wanted to have her aborted, leaving the mother she scorned with a terrible problem that had forced her into marriage with the stepfather Cecile had come to hate? I sighed inwardly, wondering if there had ever been any kind of a chance for them.

Strange, yet perhaps inevitable, that what looks like deliverance at a certain time may become the inescapable oppressive trap of later days. One could feel pretty sad for Britt, too, unloved by the woman he must see himself as having generously rescued, a woman who hadn't given him an heir. And Cecile must be a constant reminder of the man Shana *had* loved . . .

I gave myself a mental shake and asked Cecile if she'd like some hot chocolate.

That weekend the snows came, great feathery bits coming down as fast as if a giant eiderdown coverlet had been ripped open in the sky. Brilliant white lightened the gray skies, so that earth shone instead of the heavens.

Donner and Blitzen frolicked like mad things, plunging in drifts higher than their heads. Birds and animals left tracks, but the falling snow soon smoothed them over, giving a sense of space and isolation that was, for this first time at least, enjoyable.

I had been getting too much into the density of feelings and hostilities at the ranch; it was clouding my judgment and thought, which had to be retained if I were to learn the truth about Anne. Besides, though I wasn't afraid that whoever had stuck that cone under Neeka's saddle would have another go at me just yet, I was glad to relax, and not be suspicious and on guard.

That Sunday, as the huge flakes piled higher, it was good to make a big pot of chili that simmered aromatically while I tidied my living quarters and made an apple strudel, did some laundry, and wrote to Mother.

It was midafternoon before I went out on the veranda and took in the long sweeping view of the valley with its surrounding mountains looming white into the lowering skies. Only a little green on the undersides of the trees peeked out; their boughs were weighed down. Rainbow Terrace seemed, at its white portions, one with the surroundings, but the pink, yellow, and yellow-green shadings showed like Neapolitan ice cream.

I thought of Misty Basin. How would the vapors look now? Were elk and deer munching away at pines in their steam-heated banquet area? Well, I had snowshoes!

Why not try them out? I couldn't go as far as the Basin today, probably, but I could start getting the hang of them.

I already had on long thermal underwear beneath a sweater and heavy pants. I added ski pants, two more pairs of socks, my heavy parka, tied a wool scarf around my lower face and pulled on my rubberized boots. This was one tenderfoot who didn't mean to get frostbitten.

Holding two pairs of gloves, I got down the snowshoes and took them out on the veranda, fastening them on with fingers that grew awkward and numb before they'd finished the chore. I pulled on my gloves and cautiously stepped onto the snow that was level with the porch.

The soft snow sank a bit under my weight, but to my delighted surprise, I stayed erect. I ventured another step, lifting my feet enough to clear the surface. This soon grew tiring. I experimented a little, and soon found the best method was to raise a shoe just a little and slide

160

it over the other shoe's overlapping edge.

It was fun! Without the snowshoes, I'd have plunged to floundering depth. I'd have had to use my energy to pull up and put down my hole-driving feet. This way I could move along easily, though without grace. The snow was firm enough to hold Donner and Blitzen, who careened ahead of me.

I trekked around the lodge, going partway along the path to the gentian meadow, though there was no path now, of course, only a fairly regular way marked by the absence of trees and bushes. My breath, held by the wool scarf, kept my nose and chin warm, but my exposed forehead and eyes were beginning to smart.

I was turning homeward, well pleased with my first snowshoe-ing, when I heard something that sounded like a chain saw, a persistent hum that grew louder.

Out of the woods between the ranch and lodge shot an odd red vehicle that looked like a carnival bump car on skis. It was headed for the lodge when whoever was driving it seemed to spy me, checked, swerved, and then sped toward me across the white expanse.

# 17

For a moment I was overpowered by a primitive wish to run, even though that was nonsense, the driver was surely on some legitimate errand. I couldn't run, though, in the cumbersome snowshoes, and so I moved doggedly along, feeling like handicapped prey approached by some predator infinitely superior in strength and speed.

It was a relief to see Colin in the vehicle. He stopped beside me, ruffling a fine shower of snow about us, and called, "Want a ride?"

I was ready. The snowshoes called for more energy than I had dreamed they could. So I sat on the edge of the snowmobile and pulled off the inventions that had let me stay on top of the snow, then settled beside Colin, who watched me approvingly.

"I came over to see if you'd like a lesson in snowshoeing, or if you needed anything, but you beat me to it," he said. "Enjoy yourself?"

I nodded. "But I'd hate to have to get anywhere fast."

"If you do, phone, and I'll take you in this baby." He started the engine and we whirred to the lodge. "Am I lucky for coffee?" he asked, his face darkly alive against the white world.

"Sure. Come in."

He had parked near the veranda so that we could step

onto the surface. I put my snowshoes just inside the hall where they could dry slowly and led the way to the kitchen.

As I washed my hands, put on coffee, and sliced nut bread, Colin watched me so intently that I grew nervous and began to fumble. "I guess Tam is back at winter quarters," I said.

"Just in time," Colin said. "He hates snowmobiles and it's a far piece to snowshoe."

"Have you seen Cecile?"

"For a few minutes."

"Did—did you ask her about that pine cone?"

"Yes." His gaze hooded and he stared out the window beyond me. "She says she'd already left for Tam's cabin, and he agrees that she was with him by midafternoon. Still doesn't rule out a side trip on her part but—oh, I honestly don't think she did it. She's a crazy kid, and jealous, but she likes you." His gray eyes probed at me. "Are you badly upset by it? If you are, I'll rip up the floorboards to try to find out who did it, but that could stir up a lot of dust."

"What would you suggest?"

"Hell," he said, spreading his hands, "it was you who almost got your neck broken! I feel I've got a nerve suggesting anything, especially when I'm by circumstantial evidence suspect number one."

"But?"

"If we wait, we'll eventually find out who's guilty. Which might just settle a lot of things."

He spoke truer than he knew, because I was fairly sure that whoever had slipped that pine cone under the saddle had also been involved in Anne's disappearance.

"Supposing it *was* Cecile?" I asked. And I was really speaking of her possibly having done away with Anne—an act that Shana, loving her daughter, might well have contrived an elaborate deception to hide.

But Colin answered on the level concerning only me. "If things work out between you the way they promise, a fool trick in the past won't matter, will it?"

Not the pine cone, but Anne's murder?

I didn't know. All I could do was shrug. "We'll have to see. I'm not too disturbed about it, Colin. It's all right with me to go slow." I shivered slightly and grinned. "But if you do get any strong leads, you'll let me know, won't you?"

"I'll let you know."

We loitered over coffee and the nutty, rich-flavored bread till he glanced at his watch and jumped up. "Got to check on Samson's family," Colin said. "Would you like to fence tonight? Cecy phoned this morning and is keen on it. Wants to learn how to defeat Britt."

"I know. That'll take a while. But I'd be glad of company. After we're exhausted, we could make fudge or popcorn or something."

"Great!" He laughed. "We'll be over after dinner, then."

"What if Britt or Shana want to come?"

"I'll tell them we need to work with Cecy *sans* parental pressure," he said glibly, obviously having already solved that one in his mind.

The snowmobile ground hummingly away, and, after dark, returned. Colin and I worked out for Cecy, and then he gave her a lesson while I made fudge and mulled cider over cinnamon and cloves.

It was a gay evening, a fun time, oddly family-like. Even Cecile caught the mood and behaved more like a younger sister than a siren to Colin. She was also less competitive with me. It was the happiest, least tension-clouded evening I had experienced at Smoke Valley.

Yet after Colin and Cecile were gone, and I faced myself in the mirror, brushing out my hair, Anne's face seemed to superimpose itself on mine, so that I was eerily afraid for a moment and turned to look around.

I was alone except for the black dogs curled next to each other on the rug. But long after I went to bed, the fate of my sister haunted me. I reproached myself for being able to take pleasure with those who might have killed her.

I couldn't rest. Finally, I pulled on a robe and went into the registry booth, hunting through all the records for some clue to Anne. Her name was there, the date on which she started work, the date on which she left, August 8. But there was no reason given. The ledger said, "Left," not "Discharged." So I was no wiser than before. I dusted myself off and padded back to bed.

*Anne,* I vowed silently, *when I know—and I will know!—you'll be avenged. But how would you be avenged on a fourteen-year-old?* I fought my pillow and tossed and turned a long time before I got to sleep.

So as winter settled in, I became in truth the winter keeper, waiting in unearthly suspended white silence for the spring, just as I waited inwardly to learn about my sister.

Of course there *were* sounds. I came to know the difference between coyote and wolf song, to recognize the shriek of a bald eagle in the sky. I snowshoed past where an occasional pika left tracks like a small rabbit where it had ventured out, though most of the time the little creatures snuggled in their fragrant hay piles underground, munching at their swaddling in warm companionable drowsiness, a state so different from the isolated sterile sleep of the animals in Britt's laboratory that I was often tempted to sneak over and let them all out, releasing the waking ones and burrowing the slumbering ones deep in some tunnel.

Some fiction of property rights and the knowledge that any such precipitous action could sabotage my whole effort at solving Anne's mystery kept me away from the lab, but awareness of the unhappy cages lingered at the back of my mind, prejudicing my feelings toward Britt.

Not that I saw him often, but every week or so he stopped in to see how I was, and if I needed anything.

On such occasions, my wariness of him, my dislike of his attitude toward animals, could not prevent growing consciousness of him as a frighteningly attractive man, one with strong urges which souring love had forced into peculiar sidetracks. His russet gaze could shake me, and that light cultured English inflection pleased my ears, teased my senses.

I was afraid of what would happen if he touched me. He never did. Only with his eyes.

We never fenced again, either, as if we both realized that armed conflict would bring the stealthy sexual battle, waged at unspoken half-hidden levels, to an undeniable flood tide that would sweep over and perhaps destroy us. I had an intuitive certainty that he feared creating such a turbulence as much or more than I did.

Because, in spite of everything, he still loved Shana? Because of something else that had happened?

However that was, though he came to see me fairly often, he never pushed for a physical relationship. This was reassuring to a degree, but in another way it made me feel as if a mountain lion was crouching above my head, outwardly placid but gauging its time to attack.

Britt seemed to me the real winter keeper, blasted in some essential part of his being, hunting the secret of winter sleep, fascinated with that slowed, torpid life, dulled heartbeat, thickened blood, that pseudo-death.

There might even be some evangelical hope in it for him. If the animals woke, might not he?

Once when he and Shana stopped in together, our conversation moved to the mystery of why some creatures migrate and others sleep in that marvel called hibernation which lets them escape the cold and the scarcity of food.

Frogs at the bottom of mud ponds, reptiles twined into masses in rock fissures to slow down evaporation of their moisture, bumblebees in hives, bears, chipmunks, bats hanging upside down in deep caverns—all these and many more go into what Indians called the Long Sleep.

"If I could just find out what triggers it," Britt said, eyes bright and restless as he sat on the edge of a stool. "We know that cold, hunger, dark, and quiet help trigger it in natural conditions, but animals in the lab sleep, too, in light and warmth, with food close by. It's fantastic! Take America's most perfect hibernator, the woodchuck."

"Mmm," yawned Shana, stretching. "You're making *me* sleepy, love!" She poured herself more coffee.

"The woodchuck?" I prompted, annoyed with her, because I did find the riddle engrossing.

"The woodchuck breathes twenty-five to thirty times a minute in the summer," Britt explained. "The rate can shoot up to a hundred respirations when he's excited. But in winter, he may breathe only once in five minutes. His summer heart throbs eighty times a minute, sledging away at two hundred in emergencies, but in winter sleep, his blood oozes like thick molasses, powered by maybe four or five heartbeats a minute. His temperature drops as low as thirty-seven degrees, not much above freezing, and he stays like that five months or more!"

"Don't they ever freeze to death?"

"There are limits to what they can stand," he admitted. "There are no hibernators above the Arctic circle. But once all animals were cold-blooded. It seems that in winter, some can almost abandon their warm-blooded condition, stay just a little warmer than their surroundings.

Ignoring Shana's glazed stare of boredom, I asked curiously, "How do they wake up? Reverse the hibernating mechanism?"

"When it warms up in spring, say to about sixty degrees, hibernations start waking. A woodchuck's temperature can go up forty-eight degrees in less than three hours. There's a record of one whose temperature soared sixty degrees in an hour. They wake from head to tail, interestingly enough, with the blood supply to the rear held down till the brain and vital organs are back to near-normal."

"That must be a weird sensation—awake in front, asleep below!"

Britt laughed. "Well, there's a lot of shivering and panting to help equalize body temperature. The animal has to get rid of all that carbon dioxide accumulated during the winter, and his heart pumps at a wildly accelerated pace, speeding sluggish blood into a hot current."

"And all those months alseep—" I mused. "I wonder if they dream."

"They can't," Britt said positively. "There's no electrical activity, hence no dreams, in a woodchuck's brain till it reaches sixty-eight degrees. Up to then, its movements are blurred, uncoordinated, but at that temperature, the brain takes over."

"And then most animals have more sense than to worry about unsolvable peculiarities," jabbed Shana, rising impatiently, tossing back her shimmering hair.

Britt flushed. "Even you can hardly label a complex survival system that utilizes reduced metabolism, low circulation, and low body temperatures simply a peculiarity, Shana. What we're talking about verges on the secret of life itself, on the mystic, suspended animation—"

"Suspended animation?" she mocked. "Suspended life— Well, my love, you *are* an authority on that!" She changed the subject suddenly, quizzing me on Cecile's progress in geometry.

Britt stared at her, his mouth set, jaw rigid. I was both relieved and fearful when they thanked me for the coffee and departed.

Winter, like a huge, all-encompassing hibernator, moved on in white spaciousness that seemed to stretch, both physically and spiritually, forever. I did my specified chores, taught Cecile in geometry and fencing, became self-respecting on snowshoes, and several times a week enjoyed the company of Colin and Cecile for fencing and refreshments.

They were much more relaxed with each other. Cecile seemed happy to be with the man she adored, while he, able to drop his guard, could show her affection and interest.

Shana came every week or so in her white and gold snowmobile, looking, I thought, like the Snow Queen out of the fairy tale, wearing a white ermine-trimmed parka, and white boots and trousers; the only color was her golden hair, perfect skin, blue eyes, the bright stain of her mouth. She loved the winter, zooming everywhere over the white crust, exhilarated by the end of confinement to roads and ordinary routes.

"It's like flying," she told me once, eyes sparkling. "Why don't you learn? I'll teach you."

I smiled and shook my head. "I'll stick to snowshoes," I said.

She frowned. "Now you sound like that old fool, Tam Cannon."

"Have you heard from him?"

"What's to hear? Colin goes by every few weeks." She started the gold and white chariot, waved her hand, and swirled away, cresting the drifts like a surfer.

Which made me think of Anne.


When snow got thick on the roof, which it frequently did, making the shingles creak and groan with its threatening weight, Colin and some of the cowboys would come to clear it off.

One day after the crew had completed this chore, Colin asked if I'd like to ride over to Misty Basin and see the animals. That walk was too far on snowshoes with temperatures that were now often well below zero, so I accepted gladly, bundled into layers of clothing, and joined Colin in the red snowmobile. There were two other snowmobiles at the ranch: a green number shared by Cecile and the cowboys, and a black one reserved for Britt.

I regarded them with mixed loathing and admiration. There was no doubt that they were the only way to cover distance in the snow, yet I detested their sawing racket, the way they came shooting out of nowhere when I was out peacefully slogging along on what Cecile teasingly called my "tennis rackets."

Colin parked the snowmobile some distance from the Basin. "So we won't scare anything off," he explained, giving me a hand as we walked on the hard crust, sinking a little but managing without too much difficulty.

We stopped at the rise above the basin. I caught and held my breath. Scores of moose and elk fed at the lodgepole pines below or warmed themselves in vapors that steamed more densely than ever in this crystalline air. One elk played in the snow with his antlers. Some geese swam about in their heated pools, and Colin pointed out a kingfisher's brilliant plumage.

Suvi, at the edge of the geyser activity, sent up puffs of steam that disintegrated fleecily against the leaden heavy sky.

"It's like an animal resort or spa!" I whispered delightedly. "Oh, Colin, what a good idea to come! I wouldn't have missed this for worlds."

"The price won't come that high." His hand, even through our several pairs of gloves, seemed to caress my naked one. Tinglingly aware of him, I stepped back.

His eyes narrowed, but after a moment he chuckled, throwing back his head so that the hard line of his jaw was thrust forward. "Fine, Snow White. Just watch the birds and beasties—and from men and life and things that might go bump in the night, may the Lord deliver you!"

"You don't have to be so mean about it!" I snapped.

His eyes engulfed mine. I could not move. "Don't I?" he asked. He didn't touch me, just turned on his heel. "We'd better be getting back."

I followed him, finding it harder alone, somehow feeling myself to be the offending person, the one of little faith.

But how could I trust him? How?

# 18

As he helped me into the snowmobile, I heard the distant whine of another snowmobile, vibrating in the hush. We both looked in the sound's direction, but only saw the white enchantment stretched out on all sides, vaulted to the mountains.

It was impossible to talk much in the snowmobile over the engine's sound, which, considering the mood we were in, was just as well. I brooded as Colin steered expertly over our former track, then was jolted back to reality at seeing patches of color against a slope.

There was the green snowmobile, a bright cardinal-red snowsuit Cecile wore often, and a large brownish humped form. As we got closer, we could see that Cecile was bending over the big shape. She turned slowly as Colin looped around to pull up by her.

She stood up from the dead elk, tears running down her face, tears that congealed at once so that she brushed rigid crusts away. Colin climbed out and examined the still body.

No blood, no sign of injury. The elk's tined antlers proved him a mature specimen. His mane fell across his dark brown neck and his gray-brown body lay as if he had collapsed in the middle of a heap, as if his power had snapped all at once, as if his heart had simply broken, refused to run anymore.

"What happened, Cecy?" demanded Colin, bending to examine the elk, shifting it a little.

"I—I don't know. I just found him like this. But there were snowmobile tracks. See them?" She pointed to a confusion of tracks in the snow, but there was no way to tell what vehicle had made them. Her green eyes flamed. "Colin, someone must have run him to death!"

"Who's your candidate?" Colin asked drily. "You didn't see?"

"No. But people from Yellowstone get over sometimes. It might have been one of them."

"I know our men," Colin mused. "None of them would do this. Of course, whoever was in the snowmobile may have just wanted to get up closer. Maybe, if they were vacationers, they didn't know what could happen."

The girl shook her head, cupping her face with her mittened hands to warm it so that her voice came out muffled and queer. "Look at those tracks, Colin. No one could be that close on an animal for so long without knowing what they were doing."

Colin walked over the slope, disappeared for a few minutes, then returned. "It does look like a chase," he admitted reluctantly. "I'll call Yellowstone headquarters, tell them to keep an eye out for 'sportsmen.' The trouble is that in the snow, fences just don't matter. The snowmobiles coast right over what would ordinarily be a barrier." He added grimly, "Well, one can't run with a bullet in the motor, and I'll tell our men to carry rifles. We'll disable any vehicle we see chasing game. Hunting is one thing, but this—"

His mouth curved with disgust. He put an arm around Cecile, easing her into the green vehicle. "Go home now, honey. You can bet I'll try to make sure it doesn't happen again."

He waited till she was over the slope to start our engine. We followed her till she turned off to the ranch with a wave of her hand.

Seeing an animal, a magnificent strong one, dead like that would have bothered me anyway; the lack of outward violence and wounds added a secret threat, a subtle dimension of sadistic, deliberate cruelty that chilled me.

Colin's jaw was set as he steered. I wondered if he had any ideas beyond strayed vacationers from the national park. It was possible, of course, that Cecile had cruised down the elk, but I didn't believe she had. Her grief had been too poignant.

Britt? Some unsuspected oddball among the cowhands? Shana? Of them all, Britt seemed to me the most likely, but I much preferred to think the killing was done by an outsider, someone I didn't know.

Yet it was certain that, if my sister hadn't run away with Nordstrom as reported, then one if not more of these Smoke Valley people had to be involved. And if they'd kill a girl, or cover up her death, wouldn't they run an elk till his heart burst?

Colin stopped at the veranda. "Do you think you know who did it?" I asked.

"No, but I'm going to try to find out." His lips made a straight hard line and his eyes were the color of the stormy sky. "I'll alert the park rangers and warn our men to be on the watch. We'll carry rifles. Maybe—probably—whoever did it was on a one-time binge, but if they carry on with it, we'll get them sooner or later, and I hope it's soon!"

"So do I," I echoed fervently. "Can you come in for coffee?"

"No, thanks, I'm getting the men together right away, cluing them in on the fact that they've got to be on the lookout for someone kinky. If our gallant snowmobiler would run an animal till its heart failed, he might pick a man next time."

Colin had said *he*; was that usage or conviction?

I was tempted to ask if he was also going to have a talk with Britt, but the idea of anyone I really knew doing this thing was so obscene, so terrifying, that I didn't want to even imagine it till I had to.

I felt lonely and deserted after Colin pulled away. A romp with Donner and Blitzen, a hot bowl of chili, even a phone call to Mother didn't lift my sense of desolation and fear.

"You sound strange, Jan," Mother said worriedly. "Is everything all right?"

I could picture her inquiring wrinkle of the brow and longed to hug her, assure her that she still had one daughter on this earth who loved her a lot. I couldn't tell her about the elk, so I just told her I was fine and that I still didn't know more about Anne.

"But I have a feeling I'll learn soon, if there's anything different to know," I said.

"Jan, I wish you'd come home."

I wanted to, wanted to get away from this tangled place of beauty and death and secrets, but I *had* to know—about Colin as much as about Anne. "Don't worry, darling," I said. "I'm being careful. Have you seen more of Michael McShane?"

That effectively turned the subject, for, laughing a bit embarrassedly, she admitted that indeed she had, in fact he was at the house then. It made me feel better, knowing she had someone nice and solid around.

I gave her descriptions of the snow and how Misty Basin had looked that afternoon with the animals grazing and the geese enjoying their luxurious warm stream in the middle of zero weather.

"Fantastic!" Mother laughed, sounding happier. "This Colin, darling— Your voice changes on his name. You like him?"

*Love him, I'm afraid. But Mother, Mother, he may have killed Anne ...*

"He's interesting," I said, as lightly as I could.

We chattered on a while. She promised to send a book she thought I'd like, and I asked about some crewel stitches. Hearing her voice had helped while it lasted, but as soon as I hung up, the uneasy hunted feeling possessed me again.

Nonsense! I hadn't been this bothered when someone

had tried to get me thrown from my horse, when I'd seen Britt's laboratory, learned about Shana's blooding, or seen the smear of Colin's blood on her cheek. I hadn't been this jumpy when Britt walked in that first night through the unlocked upstairs door, or when Cecile had teased about shoving me into a boiling spring. There was no reason to it, no reason why the elk should have become an obsession with me, but it had. And I knew I wasn't going to breathe freely till we knew who had done it.

The wind made the lodge creak, and even the presence of the dogs couldn't keep me from jerking up from my book to listen each time some sound seemed a bit unusual. Which was ridiculous, because in the state I was in, everything sounded weird. Ghostly footsteps, doors closing, murmuring voices.

The wind. The wind and virtuoso sound effects of an old timbered lodge in the grasp of winter.

I read till my eyes kept shutting in spite of my tense nerves. Then I had a glass of milk and a tranquilizer, called the surprised but appreciative dogs upon the bed to nestle around my legs, tried deep breathing, all the relaxing techniques I'd ever heard of, and finally dropped into restless, unrefreshing sleep, filled with dreams where deer, elk, and coyotes ran from machines, laboring in the snow while featureless men grinned with fanged teeth from the vehicles.

Once Anne was the quarry. I was running, too. Gasping, panting, I saw her body, struggled on, fell, got up, fell again as a motor stopped . . .

Someone was banging at the door. I woke heavily, exhausted, still in the dream torpor. "Jan!" a man's voice shouted, so muffled that I wasn't sure whose it was. The dogs hit the floor, barking to make up for not having roused earlier. "Jan! Are you there?"

I swung out of bed, fumbled into the robe on the chair, thrust my feet into slippers, and yawned my way to the door, glancing in disbelief at the kitchen clock as I passed through.

Nine? I never slept that late!

Chagrined at finding myself about to get an undeserved name for sloth, I pushed back my hair, gave a despairing and defiant sigh about the way I must look, and called, "Who is it?"

Enough of last night's dread was in me to prevent my throwing open the door just because someone had called my name. People who knew it were probably the most dangerous. For the first time, I began to think seriously of ditching the whole game, getting out.

What would it profit my mother to lose her other child? And there were a lot of things I hadn't done yet—a world of possibilities, in fact. All these thoughts and more must have formulated during the dream-wracked night to emerge in the seconds between my question and the answer in a voice I now recognized.

"It's Britt Lindsay, Jan."

I opened the door a few inches. "Sorry," I began, "I read till all hours and slept late—" The haggard look on his face made me break off. "Is something wrong?"

"Could you come over to the ranch?" he asked. "Cecile—she's having a bad time. She found Tam Cannon dead by his cabin this morning. Looks like a heart attack."

The canny, alert, shrewd, kindly old man with his Harry Truman face?

"Tam?" My heart rejected it. "Dead? Oh, please, no—"

"I'm afraid it's true," Britt said starkly. "Colin's gone into town with the body, to make arrangements. Shana can't do a thing with Cecile, and the girl hates me, so that's no use." He said it in a matter-of-fact way, without rancor, so that I had to give him some credit for being concerned about his stepdaughter.

"Of course I'll come," I said, stepping back. "Will you wait in the kitchen?"

I dressed in a hurry, gave my hair a quick brushing, and was with Britt in five minutes. I let the dogs out, since they could always find refuge at Colin's if they got cold while I was gone. They coursed after the black snowmobile for a while, but Britt went fast, dangerously fast, it seemed to me, and we lost them before we passed Colin's place.

Britt drove with concentration, his thin delicately featured face outlined stark against the snow. Only when he pulled up in front of the house did he look at me, a long questioning gaze that held, I thought, a touch of wistfulness.

"You're a good girl," he said, the everyday formula coming strangely from his aristocratic lips. "It's been helpful to know you were here, even though we don't meet as often as I could wish. Jan, I—"

Afraid of what he might say, and equally anxious to get to Cecile, I got out of his vehicle. "Thanks for bringing me," I said, hurrying up to the big french doors where I had knocked months ago, while autumn smiled, before winter locked us in the valley, before Tam died.

Paula was waiting to let me in, her usual carved expression of imperturbability shattered with distress. "Go on up, miss." She nodded toward the staircase. "Poor Cecy, she can't stop crying and I can't get her to stop, nor her mama."

I walked past the hunting scenes, glancing unwillingly at the chilled panic in the eyes of the beautiful girl-woman in the portrait, which I now always saw with a smear of blood on the face. At the top of the stairs, I turned into Cecile's room.

She wept in a keening ugly wounded way, huddled on the floor, her bright head down. Shana, kneeling by her, tried to embrace her, but Cecile pulled away.

"Leave me alone!" she screamed. "Get away! You hated him, you know you did!"

Shana looked helplessly toward me, then rose, her hands limp as wilted flowers. "If you don't get yourself under control soon, Cecile, I shall have Britt give you a sedative."

"I won't take it!"

"You'll take an injection. We can hold you down if necessary. This howling like a savage has got to end!"

"If you didn't want a savage child, you shouldn't have messed with my daddy!"

Shana's arm flew back, but she checked the blow, staring at me with burned-out eyes that looked like the blue-painted ones of a bisque doll. She made an exasperated hopeless gesture at her daughter, then went past me without a word, going downstairs, her accustomed flowing grace distorted into the movements of a stiff-pegged marionette.

Cecile mourned on in a raw, hoarse, monotonous lament. She seemed not to know I was there. "Cecile," I murmured, "Cecile, I'm so terribly sorry. Tam was—he was a great person."

She jerked up, glared for a moment, then collapsed against my knees. "Yes, he was great! You know that, Jan! And he was—he was—oh, Jan, he really loved me! He really loved me! Not because I was his and he *had* to. He loved *me!*"

"Yes. And you loved him. A great deal. Of course you feel terrible. You will for quite a while." I hunted for words, true ones that would help. "But there'll be a time when, though you'll feel sad, you'll be glad you knew him, that such a person lived. You'll remember the fun you had with gratefulness and joy—it'll seem that he knows, too, wherever he is, and you'll feel him smiling."

"I don't believe it!"

Did I?

I thought of Anne, realizing with surprise that already I often thought of her, of things we'd done together, without that dizzying pain, resentment, and anger that had used to come. But when I wondered how she'd died—

"It is true, Cecile," I said positively. "Tam would tell you that everyone, everything dies in its season, but life goes on, and it's good. Cry for him when you need to, all you need to. Of course you'll miss him. But what he was to you can never be lost, you'll always have it built right

178

into what you are."

"It's not true! He's dead, he's gone!"

"He's dead, but he's not gone."

"Yes, he is."

"How can he be, Cecile? How can he be, when you weep for him like this?"

She looked at me for the first time, blinking. The rage on her swollen face suddenly dissolved, broke into pure grief, and she let my arms come around her, let me hold her while she sobbed, cried longingly, desperately, but without the hatred and rebellion that had tainted her mourning before.

I petted and stroked and rocked her till the sobbing dulled, till she sat up, giving me perhaps more of a push than was necessary, and blew her nose, glanced at her watch.

"Colin ought to be in town with Tam by now," she said, her voice ragged from crying but amazingly steady. "I don't see why we can't just bury him here."

"Well, the law requires a death certificate and embalming, Cecile. Otherwise people might be buried. who weren't really dead."

She mulled over that a while. "Tam was Presbyterian," she mused. "I suppose the funeral will be at the church, though I reckon Tam only got in for services at Easter. He always went then." Her eyes softened. "Once he took me. I don't like churches, but I liked that, the singing, the flowers. I hope there'll be a lot of flowers for Tam."

There were. The little Presbyterian church was banked with them, many sent from all parts of the West by old cowboy friends, a huge spray from the Stockmen's Association, the casket covering of yellow roses from Cecile. As we filed past the coffin for a last look at Tam, I saw Colin slip something under his old friend's hands, Tam's worn rawhide lariat.

Tam had preferred cremation to burial, so after Britt, Colin, Cecile, and I had accompanied the body to the crematorium, we stopped at a cafe to rest and have lunch before returning. Shana hadn't come. Cecile had forbidden it.

"In the spring we'll scatter his ashes around his winter quarters," Cecile said. "I'm glad he won't be buried here in town."

She hadn't cried during the funeral, but now she did, turning to Colin who let her burrow against his dark blue suit jacket. He reached in his pocket for a handkerchief. As he produced it, a folded paper fell out and slipped to the floor.

Since I was nearest, I bent to pick it up. It flipped open. A ticket. To Los Angeles. I fumbled with it, managing to read the dates. It was for August 11, the day we'd received the telegram about Anne, and the return was a few days later.

My heart went absolutely still. I felt as if my brain were the only operative part of a frozen body. I had to give the ticket to Colin, but absorbed as he was in comforting Cecile, he didn't look at me.

Britt was watching, though, pale wine-colored eyes intent. "Are you all right, Jan?" he asked solicitously.

I nodded, forcing a weak smile. "Could I have some more coffee, please?"

He signaled the waitress. Cecile slowly calmed again, and we had our silent meal, the quiet between the two men almost menacing, though they were civil enough in the little they said.

My brain kept whirring, but my body stayed cold, rigid with fear and dread, horror of what seemed true.

Colin had been in the area, at least, when Anne died. It was too much of a coincidence to think he had just happened to fly down there that day.

Was he Nordstrom? He must be! Shana would cover for him, certainly. She'd have been relieved in some measure to have her rival out of the way.

The only thin hope I nursed was that Anne really had drowned, that Colin and she had gone for a holiday, and she had lost her life in an accident. But then why hadn't he signed the telegram with his own name? Why had

Shana lied, affirming the existence of Lars Nordstrom?

There seemed to be no reason for such elaborate tricks if Anne's death had been an actual drowning. But though the evidence seemed horribly clear, I wanted to somehow question Colin about it, try to read his eyes before I went to any police with my suspicions. There was a chance he hadn't killed her. I put all my longing and hope in that, even as I felt the chain against my flesh beneath my blouse, the chain with Anne's ring on it.

That was it. I'd show him the ring, tell him I'd found it, watch how he reacted Maybe—maybe—oh please, God, let there be some explanation besides the one that seemed so plain!

Yet what could it be? My mind circled like a hunted beast, round and round, fleeing yet driven back to hard fact. Colin had flown to California the day Anne was reported dead.

And if he were innocent of wrongdoing beyond taking a girl on an adventure, why had he used an assumed name? Was he the Nordstrom who had checked into the lodge now and then? Was that a game he played to find new loves? Of course I couldn't be positive he had posed as Nordstrom, sent the telegram. But he *had* been near Long Beach. And if he wasn't Nordstrom, who was?

<h1 style="text-align:center">19</h1>

Colin drove Cecile home while Britt took me. We pulled up by the lodge in late afternoon. It was sub-zero, the trip from town had taken nearly three hours, and though I wanted only to be alone, I felt constrained to ask Britt if he'd like some coffee.

He followed me in, stripping off his parka, mittens, and the heavy rubber boots he'd worn over his dress clothes. I similarly disencumbered myself and put the coffee on while Britt lounged in a rocking chair I had moved into the kitchen so that I could have a change from sitting in my bedroom.

"You have a great gift, Jan," he said, just as I was beginning to grow uneasy under his scrutiny.

I raised my eyebrows, and couldn't repress a rueful smile. "Tell me about it quick!"

He frowned. "It's not to laugh at, Jan." His voice gentled. "But you would. You don't understand how rare you are."

This kind of talk was making me extremely uncomfortable. "Would you like some fruit bread?" I asked.

"Sit down!" he commanded. "I want to talk to you for a few minutes without you fidgeting around, acting like a scared deer, changing subjects." As I stared at him, he smiled coaxingly, saying in a softer tone, "Sit down, Jan, please."

He looked capable of making me if I didn't. Grudgingly, I perched on a stool on the far side of the table from him. He grinned tolerantly.

"All right, my dear. Stay behind a barrier if it makes you feel better. Just let me say what I want to." He paused, set his slim long fingers together, and considered me with his amber eyes, which seemed alight with a deep inner spark. "Jan, you have the gift, the marvelous seldom-found gift, of easing pain."

I could only stare.

"To end pain," he said. "That's why I've hunted the secret of hibernation. During a dreamless sleep like that, a man could heal from his soul wounds. But you can heal a person who's awake."

I made a disclaiming gesture, but he waved me to silence.

"Look how you calmed Cecile down three days ago. I was ready to give her a heavy sedative, I'll tell you. All that caterwauling and Shana no use at all—" His mouth constricted. "But you hushed the girl, you somehow got her to accept old Tam's demise. Knowing Cecile and her damned heathen lack of moderation, it was a miracle to me."

"I was glad to help," I said, unable to look away from him."

"Of course you were," he agreed, getting to his feet, crossing lightly to me, circling the table. "You'll always be—glad to help. Won't you?"

I wanted to get up, retreat, but besides feeling almost hypnotized by his soft voice, that smoldering excitement in his eyes, I was afraid that if I moved, he'd try to catch me.

And of that, in this strange moment, I really was afraid. For Britt appeared kind and human, and seemed to care about me. I was so bewildered and torn about Colin that the relief of being consoled by another person was incredibly tempting. I had been alone among people

I had to suspect for over three months now, tormented by the riddle of my sister's death, increasingly attracted to the man who now seemed certain to have taken some part in it.

Weak, fruitless, not to be allowed but extremely attractive was the wish to let Britt hold me, to put my face against his chest, let out the fear and sorrow in a gust of weeping. Even if I had to pay for it . . .

His hands fell to my shoulders. His mouth came down on mine, pleading softly. Kiss and embrace stayed so gentle that I could easily have freed myself.

I didn't. He lifted his head, triumph in his smile, his voice. "You will—be sweet to me, won't you, Jan? God, I need it! I need you more than that bratty Cecile does!"

Feeling dazed, as if I were somebody else temporarily inhabiting my body, I could only stare. He held my face in his hands and started to kiss me again. This time I freed myself, stepping back.

"You have a wife, Britt."

He shook his head. "Not really. She—"

"Your problems are between the two of you," I cut in quickly, before it occurred to me that any philandering proclivities Britt had might cast some light on the tangle into which Anne had vanished.

Britt, fortunately, overrode my warning. "I can't talk to her," he said bitterly. "Besides, we're past all that. She only wants to stay married to me, enjoy the money and her little pleasures. She's glad when I'm occupied elsewhere."

"Oh?" I inquired, lifting an eyebrow.

"I *am* a man," he defended. "And not all women worry about my being married." He laughed. His voice took on a note of boasting. "That was an advantage to some of them who were married, too, here at the lodge on vacation alone."

My tongue stuck to the roof of my mouth. "But isn't that a bit sticky?" I asked. "Since you own the lodge and everything—"

"But they didn't know that, Jan, you innocent!" he

said with superior amusement. "When I got really interested in a woman, I checked into the lodge under an assumed name. In a few days, I'd either had my luck or
marked it off."

I shook my head in unfeigned wonder. "Did Shana
know?"

"Of course she did." In spite of his bravado, he sounded rather unhappy. "But she much preferred over-look-
ing my indulgences than gratifying them herself. Besides,
my dear, you've heard the old one about people in glass
houses."

So he *might* have been Nordstrom. Revulsion at him
mingled with a wild hope that perhaps, after all, Colin
might not have taken Anne to California in spite of that
plane ticket. But how to find out without alerting Britt?

I gave a judicious nod, as if at his cleverness. "Yes, I
can see where an affair with a guest would be pleasant
without any ties or aftermaths. But a lot of pretty girls
work here in the summer, I gather. Weren't you ever
tempted?"

"Of course! But again, they didn't know who I was, I
was simply a lodge guest for as long as it lasted. When I
left for the ranch, they thought I was going to Michigan
or New York or wherever." He spread his hands. "No
problem."

"Apparently you're quite an expert," I couldn't resist
jabbing. "Am I your first experiment with a winter
keeper? You let me believe they were Colin's province."

"The winter is a different situation altogether," Britt
replied, with a touch of somberness. "The lodge isn't
open, it's hard to conceal identity. No, I've never played
with our winter keepers, Jan. I'm not playing with you."

I froze, alarmed at the way his voice sank as if he were
talking to himself. "What—what do you mean?" I said,
when I could force the words out.

"I don't want just an affair with you, sweet. I'd like to
marry you." His eyes half-shut and his lean handsome
face looked so sad and weary, so full of longing, that I
felt for him at the same time that I was shocked. "You

could ease my pain, Jan. I know you could. And you could give me children, someone to leave Smoke Valley to."

"Britt, you don't really mean that! You still love Shana."

"I do, but I can stop, root her out. You can fill my eyes and mind and heart."

"But—"

"Look, don't distress yourself about that woman!" He caught my hands and wouldn't let me retreat. "I'll give her a big cash settlement, enough to go live wherever she likes in high style. She won't protest long when she sees it's that or an ugly court fight." His mouth tightened. "I can prove her adultery with Colin, and I will, damn her, if she makes trouble!"

Shana might have deserved expulsion from the ranch—it didn't mean much to her anyway. But Cecile! So much a part of the swirling mists, knowing the whole region, loving it! I wouldn't have been remotely interested in Britt's proposal, even if it hadn't been for Anne, but his callous disregard of Cecile's roots in Smoke Valley made me indignant enough not to have to pretend my anger.

"I wonder how many women you've told this story to?"

He flinched as if I had slapped him and sucked in his breath. "Then," he murmured as if to himself, "we'll try it another way."

He started for me. I edged around the table, fighting panic, trying to keep my mind from flaring into blind fear. If he were Nordstrom—if he had taken Anne to California—

There was the sound of a distant chain-saw buzz, the barking of dogs. Britt seemed oblivious to everything except cornering me, moving after me lightly on the balls of his feet, ready to lunge.

We were not separated by foils, spectators or rules. I couldn't parry him for long, not if it came to strength and speed ... The motor cut off outside. I circled the table, dodging into the hall.

"Colin!" I shouted, as he knocked and came in. "I—I'm glad you brought the dogs home! It's feeding time."

"Yes, I thought I'd bring 'em home while I was mobilized," he said. "Coffee on?" His gaze moved past me to Britt, who stood in the kitchen door, uneven breathing and a slightly strained expression the only sign of what had happened.

"I'll be going," Britt said. "See you later, Jan."

He went out without speaking to Colin, who looked after him with a raised eyebrow and inquired, "What was that all about?"

What indeed?

Fortunate as Colin's appearance had been, I wished I'd had a chance to sort out my information before seeing him again. I tried swiftly, while I led the way into the kitchen and ostentatiously rattled cups and spoons, to assess what I knew.

Britt might have been Nordstrom. So might Colin. Both had been involved with women either staying or working at the lodge, and were possible suitors of Anne. But the Nordstrom lie made no sense in Colin's case unless he had killed Anne. An accident, even under those circumstances, could have been explained and accepted.

A married man on a frolic, even with his wife's tacit consent, was a different thing, though, in a case of accidental drowning. Britt *could* have taken Anne to California, she *might* have drowned, and everything in the telegram would have been true except the signature.

I hoped that was the answer. It would mean no one had committed murder. Though the waste of my sister's young life would still be tragic, it wouldn't call for vengeance beyond simply making Britt know and acknowledge the possible results of his casual affairs.

I poured coffee for Colin, some for myself, and perched on a stool, avoiding his probing look. "Britt was just telling me his troubles," I said dismissingly.

Colin snorted. "He must have been doing it pretty energetically! He looked breathless. And you seemed half a jump ahead of the big bad wolf and losing ground fast!"

My face colored, and I watched my coffee as if fascinated by it. "I've always suspected Britt played his little games," mused Colin. "Figured it was none of my business. Till now." His brown hard fingers closed on my wrist. "Did he bother you, Jan? Persist?"

"I can't see that it's any of your business."

He released me as if my flesh had suddenly burned him. His gray eyes chilled like sleet in a storm sky. "I guess not. He's handsome, a rich man. Play your cards right and he might marry you."

"Damn you, you've no right to say that!"

"I calls 'em like I sees 'em," he returned, but my outrage appeared to mollify him slightly. He surveyed me with brooding attention. "Okay," he said at length. "It's none of my business. But if you get in a bind, don't be pig-headed. I'll help you, even if you are a mean-tongued little witch!"

"Thank you indeed," I said with sugary politeness. Deciding that the best way to learn more about Colin was to pretend to be tentatively interested in Britt, I pulled the chain holding Anne's ring from under my blouse. "I wonder if this belonged to one of Britt's—friends? I found it in one of the bedrooms when I was cleaning."

"Let me see that!"

I slipped off the chain, handing it, with the ring, to him. He nestled it in his palm. I felt a searing wrench of jealousy along with shame for feeling that way about my sister. Colin had loved her. I could tell it from the way he fondled the ring.

"You found it upstairs?"

"Yes."

"Do you remember which room?"

It was better not to act too positive. "I think it was— let's see, it was on the left wing, near the exit. Room two-oh-two, I believe."

"She might have lost it while cleaning," he said under his breath.

"Do you know to whom it belonged?" I asked, trying to sound surprised and intrigued but not unduly eager.

Colin's jaw clamped tight and he got to his feet. "I think it belonged to a girl who worked here last summer—pretty kid from St. Louis. Two-oh-two, you think? I'm going to check the guest register, see who used that room last summer."

I could have told him. Nordstrom, in the last few weeks before Anne vanished. Colin looked up from the record with baffled disgust. "A string of names, none of them familiar," he said. He closed the book. If Nordstrom meant anything to him, he was doing a good job of concealing it.

The hope that he was innocent, that he had loved Anne truly, not harmed her, grew stronger in me. I wanted to ask him outright, but caution checked that, though.

He *could* be pretending, *could* be a murderer. And my mother had already lost one daughter. Colin stared at the trinket in his palm, turning to me a bit sheepishly.

"Could I keep this, Jan?"

"I was saving it for—for my kid sister," I said reluctantly.

Whether as a memento of a girl he'd adored, or as possible evidence against himself, I didn't want him to have it. But I couldn't see what good it would be as evidence, and scolded myself for jealousy. If Anne was loved and mourned by this tall man I now wanted, what right had I to grudge her his thoughts and rememberings? I straightened my shoulders.

"Oh, have it," I said, not very graciously. "You knew the girl."

He detached the ring, slipped it in his shirt pocket, and gave me the chain. "Yes, I—knew her," he said. "Her name was Anne Dupree. Sweet kid. Beautiful, honest, lively—"

That searing pang pierced me again, curved, and lingered. "You sound as if you were in love with her."

His eyes met mine. "Yes," he admitted. "I suppose I was."

"*Was?*"

He turned. I couldn't see his face. "She's dead."

My heart lurched. "How awful!" I managed to say. "Did—did it happen here?"

"No. She drowned down at Long Beach late last summer."

*Did she, by accident? Were you Nordstrom?*

He turned to me again, his face a mask. Murderer or grieved lover, how could I tell? And a mistake could cost my own life.

"Good night," he said. Hesitating, he added grimly, "I suppose you know what you're up to with Britt. Fair enough, I'll butt out. But if you do want help—" He shrugged. "Let me know."

"Well, thanks for the concern. And for bringing Donner and Blitzen home. By the way, have you learned who ran that elk to death?"

He shook his head. "No. I still have the men on alert with orders to shoot if they see anything like that."

I followed him to the big door, bolted it fast, and walked slowly back to the kitchen as the snowmobile buzzed away.

I was making a sandwich for lunch next day, depressed by Tam's funeral, the gray weather, and the riddle of Anne's death. I hoped Cecile would come for her lesson, since her chatter would at least haul me out of my apprehensive doldrums, but I doubted that she'd feel like coming over for several days at least.

I was munching in the rocking chair, giving a morsel of cheese or pepperoni to first Donner, then Blitzen, glad of their company anyway, when the familiar humming sound of an approaching snowmobile brought me to my feet.

Cecile? Colin? Britt? One of the hands?

None of these, I saw, as I looked out the window. It was Shana, in her white and gold vehicle, in her frosty white parka with the furred hood. I waved to her and ran to open the front door.

"Oh, my dear!" she cried, stamping her white-footed

feet and stepping inside. "I wonder if you'd visit Cecile today? She's terribly down, I can't do a thing with her. I suggested she come here, but she just started crying again in that terrible grinding way that has Britt banging doors and me going absolutely bonkers." She smiled imploringly. "Won't you save us?"

"I'll be glad to come," I said, finishing all the sandwich I didn't give to the dogs. "Let me get on my out door things."

I dressed in the now customary layers, tugged on boots, and joined Shana, who had waited in the cold main hall in order to have some relief from the cold without getting too hot. Deciding I wouldn't be gone more than a few hours, I let Donner and Blitzen out.

"We've got a little errand first," Shana said, as I followed her into the snowmobile. "Tam had promised Cecile his books, and she's decided she needs them. Maybe it'll make her calm down. Do you mind a quick run up after them?"

It would be out of the way to drop me at the ranch first, so I didn't know what to do but acquiesce. The snowmobile churned away. Soon we were flying over or bypassing the tortuous route we had followed before the snows.

Shana gripped the steering wheel, cheeks bright, eyes a deep liquid blue. There was a smile on her lips. She looked regal, a winter spirit, and I thought again that she was the Snow Queen.

In a wild rush of irrational fear, I gripped the edge of my seat the best I could with my awkward triple mittens. It was as if she had become that wicked ruler in the fairy tale, as if she were carrying me off to some frozen lonesome place, some midnight land lit only by the aurora borealis, and that she'd abandon me there.

I'd never get back.

*Stop it!* I told myself, forcing slow calming breaths. *This is crazy! You're just going to fetch Tam's books for Cecile.*

Yet I would have felt better if the dogs had trailed us.

They had run after the snowmobile for a while, then drifted off in the direction of Colin's. Which was doubtless a good thing since I'd be rather later getting home than I had planned.

We drew up to Tam's cabin. "Would you be a dear and run in?" Shana asked. "The books Cecile wants are on the mantel. The door's not locked. We leave it that way in case someone gets lost in the winter and needs shelter."

I climbed out, opened the door a bit edgily, moved over the rough plank floor with its variety of old rugs, and reached for the dozen or so leather-jacketed books propped on the mantel above the cheerless fireplace.

As I touched them, the snowmobile started up. The nameless fear that had been gnawing at me exploded at the sound. I dropped the books and ran for the door.

"Shana!" I called after the vanishing flash of white and gold. "Shana! Please—"

She was leaving me!

She had brought me to this deserted place, and I would freeze before I could get to safety, or starve if I tried to stay.

No one would look for me here, I thought with icy clarity. And in the spring, wouldn't it be a pity about that girl who had somehow wandered up here and died? I stood on the snow-covered step, despairing, wondering why she had done this.

Jealousy of Colin seemed the immediate answer. Or maybe she knew what Britt had in mind. My God, she had plenty of reason to kill me even without knowing that I had come to learn the truth about Anne!

Why had I ever stepped in her snowmobile?

Dread toppled over me for a few seconds. I was so afraid I couldn't think. Then I came to my senses, telling myself to go in and take intelligent stock of my situation. There could be some food, should be snowshoes, blankets, matches, firewood.

I might survive. But only if I kept my head.

As I turned, my ears picked up a new vibration in the

snowmobile's hum. I stopped and listened, and caught a deep breath.

It was coming back. She hadn't deserted me! I was so overwrought that I was jumping at fantastic conclusions. She must have just seen something and decided to investigate while I got the books.

Laughing chokily at my frantic horrors, I ran back inside and got the books, waiting with a singingly relieved heart for Shana to draw up.

But the snowmobile didn't slow down as it approached, nor did it go to the side. It was bearing right down upon me!

In the seconds before I realized what was happening, dropped the books, and ran, I caught a glimpse of Shana's face. She was still smiling, but in a frozen way, in that grimace of the painting.

My first dodge had avoided Shana's charge but carried me past retreat into the cabin. Floundering in the snow, I tried to run back to that refuge, but the snowmobile zoomed in front of me.

"Run!" Shana cried, above the sound of the engine. "Let's see you run!"

It was like a horrible slow motion movie. I ran, plunging into snow up to my waist, caught in its white soft embrace. Shana kept the snowmobile humming at lowest speed, buzzing near me like a huge insect at a trapped small one.

She whirred away. Then, tiring of her game, she looped back, coming fast this time, coming straight for me, and the snow was too deep, my feet too heavy, my blood choked my heart, thudded boiling in my skull, I couldn't move . . .

I must have blacked out for a moment before I was aware of the end of the snowmobile's noise. Opening my eyes, I stared in disbelief.

The snowmobile had stopped. Then I saw why.

Shana was slumped against the wheel. Blood stained the gold and white carriage, running into the pure white snow. And Colin was lifting me, hauling me into his snowmobile, thrusting a blanket around me while he ran over to Shana.

She was dead. Colin had aimed for the motor, but hit her. He had left her in the snowmobile, taken me to the ranch, and phoned the police, who had come out to investigate. Meanwhile, the dreadful ache in my lungs and chest had subsided.

"Shall we get a doctor out?" Colin demanded anxiously, swaddling me in quilts while Cecile brought warm milk.

I took a long sip, looked at them both, shuddered at a resurging of that nightmare chase, and said, "No, I'll be fine."

Britt, questioned by the police, seemed almost glad to tell the whole miserable perverted truth about himself and his wife, about what had happened to Anne.

"I didn't kill that girl, I never killed anyone!" he insisted. He shot Colin a vindictive look. "Apparently my noble cousin fell from honor enough to make love to my wife at least once or twice. She didn't want to end it, though he must have. Anyway, Shana was crazy jealous because Colin had an eye for this Dupree kid. One day Shana passed her in the jeep and she swore it happened before she knew it—that she hadn't really meant to hit Anne. But she did, and the girl was dead." He made nervous balls of his hands. "She was dead, nothing could change that, and Shana threatened me—"

"How?" asked an officer. "What had you done, Mr. Lindsay?"

Britt ran his tongue over his lips. "I—I'm a scientist, you know."

"No, Mr. Lindsay, we didn't," said the lawman, a blunt-jawed, heavy-browed man with a brown outdoor skin and keen hazel eyes. "We reckoned you were a cattleman, same as your daddy and his dad before him."

That nervous tongue twitched over Britt's lips again. "I studied biology and chemistry at State. You can check the records!"

The men, men of his own region, only watched him with hard eyes. "I—I conducted experiments," he said desperately. "Trying to find the secret of hibernation, solve the answer of pain, a way to stop it for long periods by a deep, deep, sleep. Think what a blessing—"

"He amputated a squirrel's leg!" Cecile cried. "Colin made him stop that kind of thing."

"But it didn't move, did it?" Britt asked in triumph. "And only a little slow thick blood oozed out! A perfect anesthetic!"

The officer cut in, disgust flaring in his eyes. "What do these—experiments—have to do with concealing a murder, Mr. Lindsay? Get to that, please."

"My wife said she'd make me look like a crazy pervert, a sadist, a madman who ought to be locked up. And I—I have needed treatment several times. She could have found witnesses like my dear bastard cousin here who'd have every reason to wish me safely in a padded cell so he could enjoy my ranch, all I have."

The officer was writing quickly. "So, in effect, when your wife told you she had accidentally hit this girl, rather than report it as manslaughter, you two decided to cover it up?"

"Colin loved the girl," Britt snarled. "He'd never have believed it!"

"I didn't believe the tale you came up with, either," Colin said grimly. "I flew down to L.A. as soon as I heard Anne had gone off with some mysterious playboy guest. But I couldn't find him, and while I was hunting, Anne's body was found." He eyed Britt carefully. "That burr under Neeka's saddle—did Shana do that?"

Britt nodded miserably. "She was jealous of Jan, too. I told her I'd kill her if she tried another trick like that!"

"So," continued the officer, "to avert suspicion and explain the matter to the girl's family, you invented a fictitious employee's prize, sent her mother a telegram in her name, drove to Long Beach with the body, put it far out in the water, sent another telegram about the 'drowning,' and came back to Smoke Valley."

Britt nodded miserably, staring at his hands which he clenched and unclenched. "Yes," he said, almost inaudibly. "That's how it was. I packed dry ice around her body in the trunk and drove like crazy—I would only doze now and then for a few minutes. And when it was safe, I put her in the water."

The officer closed his notebook. "Come with us, Mr. Lindsay. I'm arresting you as an accomplice after the fact of murder."

When I phoned mother to tell her about Anne, a deep male voice answered the phone. It was Michael McShane. I told him and knew, though I couldn't see, of course, that his arms were around my mother, that he was comforting her as I talked with her. She sounded fairly composed. It was my voice that kept breaking, but all of a sudden McShane took over the line.

"Your mother's torn up, Jan, but try not to worry. I'll take care of her."

That was good to know. I couldn't just walk out of Smoke Valley, not till some things were set straight.

The police let Britt go to his room for his personal belongings, one waiting at the door. Britt went into his bathroom and never came out. When they broke in the door, they found he had injected an air bubble into his veins.

Before that day ended, Cecile and I turned the waking animals in his laboratory loose and stowed the sleeping ones into safe locations.

Cecile was shattered at one level by her guilt over her mother's death—there had been some love there in spite of everything but she seemed happy and eager in a deeper way, released from the tortured, confused maze of congealed hate and cruelty her family had locked her in. The problem of where she was to live arose one evening.

"Paula does a great job," mused Colin, "but a girl her age needs more guidance and understanding than I for sure can give." He didn't mention Cecile's passion for him, though I was sure that was in his mind as strongly

196

as it was in mine. "Maybe another woman living in? . ."

A woman he might love? He hadn't spoken romantically to me since that last angry scene in the kitchen. I had regretfully, achingly concluded that when he learned I was Anne's sister, he'd marked off his attraction to me as a vestige, a shadow of his love for her.

"Well," I suggested, "I suppose you want me to finish out the season as winter keeper. If Cecile would like to, she can live with me till spring. Then maybe she'd like to go back to St. Louis, stay with my mother and go to high school."

He shook his head. "Don't think that would do." He lifted his voice. "Cecile!"

"Here!" she called, leaning over the banister from her room.

"Where do you want to live?"

She came down the stairs, looking from one of us to the other. "Well, here, of course!"

"But how will we manage that?" he asked. "You need a woman, not a mother, but someone older to get you through the rapids a man can't understand."

She shook her golden Afro, staring at us in scorn. "You can't figure that one out?" she asked, with a curl of her lip. "Well—"

Imperiously, she took my hand, thrusting it into his. "You two have to get married, of course! And you can adopt me if you want to, or if you don't want me here, I'll move into Tam's cabin."

Colin's hand gripped mine when I tried, blushing, to back away. "How do you feel about adopting a big daughter like that?" he asked. "Of course, we'd have to get married first. Prove we were worthy and all that!"

Cecile hooted before her green eyes grew wet. She gave me a quick fierce kiss, then ran back upstairs. I shut my eyes, waiting for Colin's mouth.

It didn't come.

Was something wrong? He surely wouldn't marry me to get a woman for Cecile! Or would he? My eyes flew open. He was grinning, a wicked glint in his gray eyes.

"Well?" he said.

"Well?" I echoed.

"I told you you'd have to ask for your next kiss."

For just a second, I glared. Who did he think he was? But I knew, I knew! He was the man I loved. And all I had to say was, "Please—" before he stopped my words.